The Baseball Card Kid

The Baseball Card Kid

Adam Osterweil

PICTURES BY Craig Smith

Front Street
Honesdale, Pennsylvania

For the children of Springs

ACKNOWLEDGMENTS

I would like to thank Leland Muller, Todd Bergquist, Noah McAskill, Ricky Schlussel, Steven Bahns, Frank Grande, Kelly Kalbacher, Raymond Hackebill, Michael Rawleigh, Joseph Gambino, Carlos Solis, Jack Hodgens, and Cindy Feldman for read-testing this book during the draft stages, and for the inspiration and encouragement they gave me throughout the writing process.

Text copyright © 2009 by Adam Osterweil
Illustrations copyright © 2009 by Craig Smith
All rights reserved
Printed in China
Designed by Helen Robinson

Library of Congress Cataloging-in-Publication Data
Osterweil, Adam.
The Baseball Card Kid / Adam Osterweil ; pictures by Craig Smith. — 1st ed.
    p. cm.
Summary: Brian and Paul venture back in time to try to rescue a collectible
baseball card on the *Titanic* before the boat sinks.
ISBN 978-1-59078-526-3 (hardcover : alk. paper)
[1. Time travel—Fiction. 2. Baseball cards—Fiction.
3. *Titanic* (Steamship)—Fiction. 4. Friendship—Fiction.]
I. Smith, Craig, ill. II. Title.
PZ7.O846Bas 2009
[Fic]—dc22
2008019216

Front Street

An Imprint of Boyds Mills Press, Inc.
815 Church Street
Honesdale, Pennsylvania 18431

The Baseball Card Kid

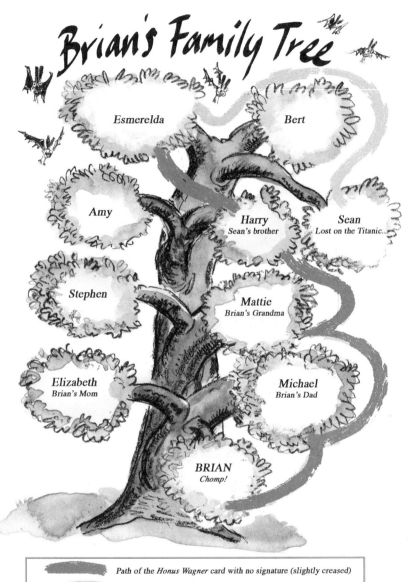

Brian's Family Tree

Esmerelda

Bert

Amy

Harry
Sean's brother

Sean
Lost on the Titanic...

Stephen

Mattie
Brian's Grandma

Elizabeth
Brian's Mom

Michael
Brian's Dad

BRIAN
Chomp!

Path of the *Honus Wagner* card with no signature (slightly creased)

Path of the mint-condition *Honus Wagner* card with signature

Paul and I Make an Amazing Discovery

Daddy opened his closet and dragged out the old wooden treasure chest, the one he always talked about in his bedtime stories. The beat-up chest had a rusty broken lock whose key had been lost in the Arabian Desert a thousand years ago. Pirates had made big gashes in its side when they buried the chest on a tropical island. It had been lost at sea when the Titanic *sank, stowed in the dusty basement of Dracula's castle, and even sent into outer space on a dangerous voyage.*

"I'll tell you a new bedtime story tonight," Daddy said, sliding the chest over to the edge of the bed, where I sat on Mom's fluffy pillow.

"I want a mad scientist to have the treasure chest this time."

"As you wish—it will be filled with beakers of mysterious bubbling chemicals. One of them can even turn a boy into a monkey!"

"He must be stopped!" I slammed my fist on the pillow and frowned at Daddy.

7

He giggled, then carefully opened the treasure chest. A pile of colorful toys sat inside. One by one Daddy took them out—an old teddy bear with one glass eye, a shiny space pistol, a metal robot, a board game covered with farm animals. Finally, he took out a small plastic case and placed it on the edge of the bed.

"Don't touch." He slowly opened the plastic case and slid a small card onto the white sheet. It had an orange background and showed a rosy-cheeked man wearing a gray shirt. "It is a very special baseball card that Grandma Mattie gave me way before you were born," Daddy said.

"Baseball card," I said, pointing at it.

"Yep, Honus Wagner, the greatest player of all time. I could retire off this if it weren't for that small crease." He pointed to a corner of the card. I leaned over to look, but I couldn't see anything. "Maybe some day. I bought a new protective case for him—a Lucite case with an etched border that was very tastefully done. Honus deserves it."

"Can I have his old house?" I asked, staring at the empty plastic case next to the baseball card.

"Sure, I don't need it anymore." Daddy turned around to get the new case. I happily grabbed for the plastic case. I stuck it in my mouth to see if it was tastefully done like the new Lucite case. When Daddy turned back around, he made a weird face.

"Honuth Wagnah, Honuth Wagnah," I said, continuing to show off how much I knew.

"No, Brian! No!" He leaped onto the bed and tried to

pull it out of my mouth, but I bit down in surprise. That's when I realized that I had accidentally grabbed the baseball card. My heart pounded, and I started crying while Daddy screamed, "Noooooooooooo!"

I woke up sweating on my top bunk. Paul stood on the ladder and shined a flashlight on my face. I sat up and remembered the nightmare—Dad's scream still seemed to echo through the house, even though the baseball card incident had happened nine years ago.

"You had the dream again?" Paul asked.

I nodded. He jumped off the ladder and turned on the bedroom light, making me shield my eyes from the brightness. I don't know why Paul still sleeps over, since I always keep us up half the night with dreams of my horrible past. It had been over a year since our whole *Comic Book Kid* adventure, and we were no closer to fixing my problem. I guess he's a true friend.

"Maybe you could get in the *Guinness Book of World Records* for being the dumbest kid ever and then use the cash to buy a new card," Paul suggested, flipping through the baseball-card price guide.

"Thanks."

"Listen to this," he continued, reading from the chapter on the world's most valuable baseball cards. " 'A mint-condition Honus Wagner T206 card from the 1909 Piedmont series recently sold on eBay for over a million dollars! Only a few hundred of these cards were ever produced, and only a handful remain in existence today, most of them in poor condition.' "

"Dad's wasn't mint because of a crease in the corner, but it would probably be worth at least half a million today."

"Cool. That's like if you ate your house AND my house," Paul said.

"Ever think about becoming a therapist?" I said angrily. Paul grabbed a yellow marker and drew a smiley face on the book's cover, with the words "Cheer up, homey" underneath.

"Look, we managed to get *Superman #1* in mint condition back from 1939," he said, tossing away the price guide and grabbing the TimeQuest comic book, the one that helped us travel through time on our comic book adventure. He flipped through it—every page was filled with colorful drawings of me and Paul on our journey. "Dinosaurs, aliens, robbers, prehistoric warriors, and futuristic technology were no match for us. We'll get another Honus Wagner card, too, somehow."

"How? That TimeQuest comic's all finished, and we don't have any way of getting another one." I hopped off the top bunk and sat next to Paul while he rambled on about our old adventure. I had been so happy after that journey, thinking that my dad didn't hate me anymore because I replaced his *Superman #1* comic book that I had wrecked when I was little. The only problem was that we accidentally altered the past during our journey, making it a baseball card that I wrecked, not a comic. The nightmares started a few weeks later, and they've become real memories now.

Suddenly, a red light flashed from the back cover of the TimeQuest comic. An advertisement appeared showing two boys flying a giant reptile into the sunset:

IS YOUR TIMEQUEST COMIC
ALL USED UP?
ARE YOU TIRED OF BEING STUCK IN
THE PRESENT TIME ... AGAIN?
THEN SEND AWAY FOR
A TIMEQUEST 2 COMIC BOOK TODAY
AND GO ON A BRAND-NEW
TIME-HOPPING ADVENTURE!

It's even better than the first because now you can warp to any*time* AND any*where* using our programmable TimeQuest bracelets!

★★For the low price of only 10 purple coins★★

Disclaimer: Traveling to the past can cause serious and lasting changes to the present. Use common sense while in the past—do not speak to anyone, leave any personal possessions behind, touch anything, breathe, or move—that is, unless you are using our experimental No-Change™ technology. Also, never, *never* eat grapes while warping through the space-time continuum (however, raisins are OK). Have fun! (Copyright 100,000 A.D.)

Paul and I stared at each other with wide eyes as a mail-order form appeared at the bottom of the page.

"See, I told you there would be an easy way to get another Honus Wagner card," Paul said. "All we have to do is go back to 1909 and get one."

TimeQuest 2 Mail-Order Form

••

Name: _____

Species Identification Password:_____

Address or Quadrant Symbol: _____

_____

Planet Subnet Code:_____

Planet Year: _____

Do you want grax with your order? _____

••

Instructions: Fill out this form using only a number 2 pencil, cut along the dotted lines, and mail to the following address along with your payment of 10 purple coins: *TimeQuest 2 Inc., TimeQuest Beach, Earth 2, 100,000 A.D.* Be sure to use TimeLeap postage if you are mailing this from a year other than 100,000 A.D.

"Oh, sure, real easy," I said sarcastically, frowning at Paul. "How are we going to mail something to the year 100,000? TimeQuest 2 comics won't be available until then, remember?"

"I have it all under control," Paul said confidently.

We Send Away for a
TimeQuest 2 Comic Book

While my parents slept we snuck down to Dad's office with flashlights and searched for supplies. Beams of light danced around the dark room as we fumbled through the desk and cabinets. I didn't really believe we could mail something into the future, but it gave me enough hope to take my mind off my horrible nightmare. That is, until Paul found the glass dome with the remains of the Honus Wagner card in it.

"Wow, you can see the teeth marks," Paul said, eyeing the ruined baseball card.

In clear black letters Honus's jersey read "Pittsburg" with no "h" on the end, but his head was bitten off—like the Headless Horseman minus the horse. Uh, and the pumpkin. Whatever.

"My dad never told me another treasure chest story after that night." I grabbed the dome and shoved it back in the drawer.

Our search turned up a big yellow envelope, a pair of

scissors, and a number 4 pencil.

"We have a problem already," I whispered, showing the pencil to Paul. "This is a number 4 pencil. The instructions say to use a number 2 pencil." I pointed to the tiny digit near the eraser.

"Great adventurers don't panic over little problems." Paul grabbed the pencil and cracked it in half, then handed the pointy part back to me. "One number 2 pencil, ready for action. Now let's head back up and fill everything out."

As I sprinted out of the office, my flashlight shined on a small book jammed behind the file cabinet. Curious, I pulled it out and dusted it off. The cover was made of thick brown cardboard and had the words "Property of Mattie" written in the center. "DO NOT TOUCH!" was written in big letters at the bottom. I quickly flipped through the yellowed, crackly pages. It was Grandma Mattie's diary!

"She gave the Honus Wagner card to my dad originally," I said, trying to read the ancient handwriting. Every page of the book was packed with tiny words in faded pencil. "Way back when my dad played baseball in high school."

"Bring it," Paul said. "It might come in handy."

When we got back to my room we placed everything neatly on the floor—Mattie's diary, the envelope, the pencil, and the pair of scissors. Then I carefully cut the futuristic order form out of the old

TimeQuest comic. Filling it out was easy because Paul told me everything to write:

••

Name: _Brian and Paul_

Species Identification Password: _Humans_

Address or Quadrant Symbol: _13 Gardiners Avenue_
_____ _Springs, NY 11937_

Planet Subnet Code: _Earth_

Planet Year: _2002_

Do you want grax with your order? _Yes, definitely_

••

"Do you even know what a grax is?" I asked, sliding the order form into the envelope.

"No, but we might need it."

"OK, so we filled out the order form," I said, carefully addressing the envelope. "That was the easy part. We still need ten purple coins and TimeLeap postage."

Paul grabbed our old TimeQuest comic and pointed to a small purple rectangle pasted onto the back cover. I took a magnifying glass out of my desk and looked at it carefully—it showed a picture of an Egyptian pyramid, an ancient Greek temple, a World War II submarine, and a futuristic city. A mailman flying a small spaceship delivered mail to each time period. The tiny words "TimeLeap Postage—one pound flat rate" spanned the bottom of the stamp.

"This TimeQuest comic was never mailed. Remember? Nathan delivered it to the General Store in person, where we got it. This stamp hasn't been used yet." Paul blew on his fingers, pretending to cool them down.

"Oh yeah, you're a genius!" Excited, I neatly cut out the stamp and taped it to the upper right-hand corner of the envelope. "But what about the ten purple coins?"

"Give me a pair of your underwear."

"What?"

"We don't have ten purple coins, so we have to give them something that weighs less than one pound in exchange for the comic book," Paul explained. "By the time the year 100,000 comes around, your underwear will be a valuable antique."

"Do you have any idea what will happen if my parents find out I'm trying to mail my underwear into the future?" I grabbed clean underwear out of my dresser and threw it at Paul's face.

"The same thing that will happen to me when they find out I told you to do it." He used the broken pencil to lift the underwear off his head, then deposited it carefully in the envelope.

"I'll bet you a grax that we never get a TimeQuest 2 comic," I said, sealing the envelope with extra-strong packing tape. I placed the finished parcel neatly on the floor, and then we stared at it for a long time while crickets chirped outside.

As dawn's light peeked over the horizon, I snuck across my lawn and jammed the envelope into our mailbox, lifting up the outgoing mail flag before dashing back inside. Paul was already asleep on the bottom bunk when I returned, so I climbed up to my bed and stared at the ceiling. I wondered if Dad would start telling me treasure chest stories again if I replaced his baseball card—I never did find out what happened to that mad scientist who wanted to turn boys into monkeys. Or was thirteen too old for bedtime stories?

We Plan Our Journey

At breakfast Paul ate Cheerios with his eyes closed. I stared groggily through the window at the outgoing-mail flag that was still up on the mailbox. It was only a matter of time before Mom and Dad determined that I was nuts.

"Brian, your hair looks less orange today," Dad said, pouring a bowlful of bran flakes. "Is something wrong?"

"That's getting old, Dad."

"I guess I need a whole new collection of jokes now that you're a teenager." He casually shined his spoon on his bald head. Dad lost most of his hair in the past year, and Mom's been complaining because it keeps clogging the bathroom drains.

"Today is a perfect day for you and Paul to weed the front lawn," Mom suggested. Paul suddenly opened his eyes. My parents recently developed this idea that slave labor will make me a more responsible teenager.

"Well, we *were* planning to do that," I said, further scrambling my eggs. "But we're morally against killing defenseless life forms that can't fight back." I shoved a piece of bacon in my mouth.

"Tell you what," Dad said, reaching into his pocket. "I'll flip a coin. Heads, you two weed the lawn, tails you wash my car." I imagined him adding, *"And if it lands on its edge maybe I'll forgive you for destroying my most prized possession!"*

Dad flipped the coin in the air. The first time it landed in Mom's coffee, but the second time it came up tails. Car wash, bleh.

"Don't forget to wear gloves," Mom said. "You never know what germs are lurking on that car."

"C'mon, it's not fair," I said. "Paul's our guest. It would be rude to make him work." Paul showed a smile full of braces to Mom.

Suddenly, a bright flash came from outside. At once my hair uncurled and stood on end. Everything on the table—the silverware, bowls, Dad's coin—tilted up and pointed to the ceiling! A loud zap from the front lawn was followed by a deafening crash.

We dashed out the front door. The mailbox was gone, and the wooden pole sizzled and gave off a trail of smoke. The bushes, weeds, grass, and dirt were scattered everywhere, mostly on Dad's car. Paul and I looked at each other with wide eyes.

"How did lightning come out of a clear blue sky?"

Mom marveled, picking up a small piece of the TimeQuest envelope.

"No need to weed, but you can still clean my car," Dad remarked.

Paul and I sat on my bedroom floor, piecing together fragments of the TimeQuest envelope.

"I'll tell you what went wrong," Paul began. "When it got too hot in that mailbox, your cootie-covered underwear exploded."

"Very funny. We didn't find any of the underwear *or* the order form."

"Look at this." He held a small piece of the envelope containing the TimeLeap stamp. A shiny holographic circle covered most of it, flashing the word "Canceled."

"The Time-Traveling mailman picked up the stuff! We did it!" I threw pieces of the envelope in the air, and they rained down like confetti. Then I thought about the futuristic customer service representative seeing what we sent, and my excitement died down. "Do you think we'll really get the TimeQuest 2 comic?"

"With your briefs and my brains, we're unstoppable." Paul grabbed Grandma Mattie's diary and started flipping through it. "Now we have to plan our journey."

"What's to plan? We go back to 1909 and buy a Honus Wagner card," I argued. "This time it'll be easy because we'll bring back coins that say 1909 on them, so we don't have the same problem as last—"

"Listen to this," Paul interrupted. He read aloud from the diary:

"May 29, 1940

Dear Diary:

Today, Father gave me a rare baseball card to add to my collection. It depicts Honus Wagner, a famous shortstop for the Pittsburgh Pirates. At bedtime, he told me the history behind the card, which I will relate here for all posterity.

In 1909 Father acquired the card from his mother, Esmerelda, my grandmother. She found two Honus Wagner cards in a single package of tobacco that she purchased at the general store for five cents. One of them had a small crease in the corner, and this one she gave to my father. The other was in perfect condition, and even had Honus Wagner's signature on it! This one she gave to my uncle Sean, whom she always favored because of the limp he received from a rare disease called Miasma Corrosus.

Three years later, tragedy struck. Esmerelda had taken Sean on a tour of Europe for his twelfth birthday. They were to return on the grand steamship Titanic, *the largest and most luxurious ocean liner in the world. Alas, the ship hit an iceberg en route to New York and sank. Grandmother and Uncle Sean perished, along with Sean's prized Honus Wagner card. Poor Sean, so unhealthy and miserable during his short life on Earth.*

Father went on to say that I must take good care of my Honus Wagner card to keep the spirit of his brother Sean alive. I must pass it along to my children, and they their children, all the way down through eternity … or at least until some fool child eats it."

"I never knew my father had a great-uncle named Sean," I said, grabbing the diary from Paul to see if what he had read was really true. It was all there—except for those last few words, which I had imagined.

"Now we have a real problem," Paul said. "I forgot they sold baseball cards in tobacco packages back then. Only adults are allowed to buy that stuff."

"Yeah, that's why so few T206 Honus Wagner cards were ever made. Honus made them stop because he didn't want kids trying to buy tobacco to get his card."

"I don't want to go to jail in 1909," Paul said. "They had rats and snakes. Anyway, we don't even know which packs will have the card. They're too rare. We need a plan B."

"Well, we can't go back and get Mattie's card. Then Dad'll never get it because we'll have messed up the space-time continuum again."

"And Sean's baseball card goes down on the *Titanic*," Paul added. "I'm allergic to icebergs."

"Well, we have to think of something!"

In English class the next day, Mr. O read us a story about a man who goes back in time to hunt a *Tyrannosaurus rex*. While he rambled on about it, I wrote a note to Paul about our plans. I wasn't convinced we'd ever get the TimeQuest 2 comic, but I had fun thinking about all the new adventures we could have with it.

"'A Sound of Thunder' by Ray Bradbury illustrates an important concept in time travel theory," Mr. O lectured. "The *butterfly effect*. Can anybody tell me what that is?"

"It's when you make a really small change in the past that results in a huge change in the future," Amelia answered. "Like when the *T. rex* hunter accidentally stepped on the butterfly in prehistoric times and that changed the president in the year 2055."

"Exactly. Very good, Amelia."

"But wait," Paul blurted. "Isn't the hunter making a change in the past when he shoots a *T. rex*? Couldn't that change the future?" Paul was actually paying attention for once. I folded my note into a little triangle and waited for the perfect moment to toss it to him.

"I know," Amelia sang, raising her hand. "The hunters went back to the time just before dinosaurs went extinct. The *T. rex*es are going to die soon anyway, so hunting one won't make the future change." I tossed the note to Paul—it landed on his desk, slid right across it, and fell into the middle of the aisle next to him.

"Thank you, Amelia. That's one way of thinking about it, but—"

"When are we ever gonna need to use this butterfly effect stuff?" Austin interrupted.

"Right now," Mr. O said, picking up my note. "This errant note is a perfect example of the theory. If I send Brian down to the office for throwing this note, he might have to spend this afternoon in the detention room, where he will reflect on what he has done and no doubt feel guilty." My face suddenly felt warm. "Perhaps he will think twice about such behavior in the

future and transform into a responsible student, and subsequently, a model citizen. When he grows up he will pass on this positive behavior to his children, one of whom might become president some day.

"However, if I ignore what he's done and throw this note out, Brian will continue to behave badly, grow up with a weak sense of morality, and his children might become criminals. Don't you see, every little thing we do could lead to a chain reaction in our life that we're not even aware of! Now imagine that chain occurring over hundreds, thousands, or millions of years. That

is the butterfly effect!" I wanted a big hole to open in the floor and swallow me and the desk. "Thank you, Brian." Mr. O handed the note to Paul while I looked around in confusion.

A few minutes later Paul threw a note back to me. It read:

Bri—

Plan B. We have 2 go back in time and get Sean's Honus Wagner card—the 1 that sinks on the Titanic. that card's going 2 be destroyed anyway so taking it out of the past won't affect the future at all. we don't want 2 risk changing things like we did with Superman #1 becuz of the butterfly effect and all. and duh we don't have to worry about icebergs because we'll just warp home before the ship sinks. btw nice timing on the note throw b4.

—Paul

We Have an Unusual Visitor

By the end of that week, I had given up on the idea of ever receiving a TimeQuest 2 comic. If it was sent from the future, we should have received it only a few seconds after the mailman picked up our package. To make matters worse, my underwear was now floating around in the space-time continuum! Paul remained stubbornly convinced that his plan would work. Friday night we played Pictionary in the den against my parents—part of their "quality time initiative."

"Broccoli?" I guessed, staring at Paul's sloppy drawing.

"Time's up," Mom chimed.

"It's a sailboat, duh," Paul said, tossing down his number 4 pencil.

"That reminds me, Dad. How come you never told me you had a great-uncle named Sean who went down on the *Titanic*?"

"How did you know about that?" He looked at me and scratched his head with his pencil.

"I read about it in Grandma Mattie's diary. I, uh, found it when I was in your office … uh, for a really good reason." After our last adventure, I told Paul that I would never lie again because it got us into a whole lot of trouble. I made Paul promise not to lie anymore either, but he broke it after about five minutes.

"I didn't want to depress you," Dad answered. "His life was cut short. I just know that he had a disease with no cure, and he was very picky about food."

"He had the other Honus Wagner card, the one with Honus's signature on it, right?"

"Yes, what a rare and special find that was," Dad said, his head drooping. "But apparently those cards were cursed."

"Our turn," Mom sang, picking up the pencil. She turned over the Pictionary hourglass timer and drew a straight line on the paper.

"Yosemite National Park!" Dad guessed.

"Correct! We win!"

"What!" I shouted. "That's just a line. You must have cheated!" It made me sick that Mom and Dad were so good at board games.

"Maybe you two should spend less time on the Internet," Mom said, giving Dad a high five.

Just then I heard a loud knock on the front door.

"Who could that be on a Friday night?" Dad asked.

"It's probably the police; they know you cheated." I ran out of the den and opened the front door. An enormous robot with glowing red eyes stood on the porch holding a brown box. The robot's bulky metallic limbs glinted in the hall light.

"Special delivery for Brian and Paul," the robot droned.

"I-I-I'm Brian," I stuttered as my knees shook.

"Sign here." A holographic delivery form appeared in the air, and my index finger began glowing. I signed my name E.T.-style, and then the form disappeared with a computerized beep. "Sorry about your mailbox," the robot added, handing me the brown package. "I was being chased by interdimensional pirates during pickup." The robot transformed into a spaceship and sped off into the night sky. My hair stood on end briefly.

"We got our package!" I yelled to Paul, running back into the den. Paul stared at the brown box. Mom and Dad looked at me suspiciously. "Uh, it's a comic book."

"You don't collect comic books," Dad said.

"Uh, I used to, in a past life. We gotta go. Good game." It *wasn't* a lie, at least. We ran to my room and tore open the package. I pulled out the letter. It read:

Dear Brian and Paul:

Thank you for ordering a TimeQuest 2 comic from TimeQuest 2 Inc. Your payment of vintage underwear from the third millennium A.D. was insufficient to *cover product delivery. On the current auction market, your underwear fetches only 9 purple coins, one coin short of the purchase price. However, we have decided to send you a TimeQuest 2 comic anyway, complete with your side order of grax. Please note, however, that your DNA has been extracted from the underwear and placed in our I.O.U. file for the amount of one purple coin, with 10% interest compounded daily. If you have any questions regarding this matter you may contact us on the neural-thought network at the following synapse: 1z4356b721365z000a*!-4.*

Happy Adventuring!
Your friends at TimeQuest 2 Inc.
TimeQuest Beach
Earth 2
100,000 A.D.

"We got it!" Paul shrieked. He pulled a shiny comic book out of the box. The gold words "TimeQuest 2" spanned the top of a shiny silver cover. Most of the cover was a metallic blank sheet, but when I looked closely, a three-dimensional moving world opened up within, showing thousands of children having adventures—running from dinosaurs, climbing pyramids, swimming through Atlantis, sailing with Christopher Columbus, all the way into the distance.

"Look," I said, pulling a small carton labeled "Grax"

out of the box. "Now we can find out what these are." I flipped open the lid, revealing a pile of green stalks that gave off a sweet oily smell. "Futuristic french fries!"

Paul grabbed a handful, jammed them into his mouth, and made loud chewing noises. "They're good!" I tried to take one, but he swatted my hand away. "You bet me the grax that we wouldn't get the comic, remember?"

"Not even one?"

"Fine, you can have that small crusty purple one."

"Thanks, Mr. Generous," I sneered. A burst of energy surged through my body when I popped it into my mouth. Drool dripped onto my chin as I watched Paul devour the rest of the fries. As he continued the feeding frenzy, I flipped through the comic, which

was filled with dozens of pages of empty comic book panels and a thin metallic sheet in the center labeled "TimeQuest Bracelets." The very last page was filled with instructions:

TimeQuest 2 Comic Book Instructions

Step 1: Put on your voice-activated TimeQuest 2 bracelet by chanting the phrase "Wear bracelet." All those wishing to time-travel must complete this step.

Step 2: Chant the DATE, YEAR, and LOCATION you wish to travel to. All bracelet wearers will immediately be transported. Note: You must pick a location within the known universe. Picking a location outside the universe could result in a malfunction.

Step 3: To return to your starting point, simply chant the word "Home." Note: Once you visit a time period, you may not return to any date within fifty years of that period using your TimeQuest bracelets, but you may always travel home. Each of the comic's five bracelets will be programmed with a HOME time and location corresponding to where your journey begins. This may not be reset or changed.

Introducing the *optional* NO-CHANGE feature!

We are pleased to announce an exciting new feature in TimeQuest 2 designed to prevent the destruction or alteration of the universe while using our merchandise—the NO-CHANGE option. After warping to a time period, simply eat a grax and chant the words "No Change" if you want to prevent changing anything in that time period. This will eliminate the risk of altering the course of history.

Disclaimer: If you ordered the optional box of grax, please note that they do not function at your HOME location. Keep them refrigerated as long as possible. We are not responsible for lost or spoiled grax or those eaten by a piggish person. As an emergency measure, each grax box contains a small crusty purple one that nobody would normally eat. This one functions just like all the rest and can prevent all space-time changes.

"Paul, stop eating those!"

He looked at me cross-eyed and let out a long burp. "Too late." He held the empty box upside down and spilled a few crumbs.

"Great. Those could have stopped us from changing history."

"Not to worry, for I have done the ultimate packing job to be ready for our journey." He dumped out the contents of his knapsack. "One bag of money from 1909, so we can buy the Honus Wagner card from

Sean. One historic map of the *Titanic*. One Lucite plastic baseball card case. One portable DVD player—"

"What's that for?"

"In case we get bored we can watch movies instead of messing up the course of history."

"All right, let's get this over with." I flipped to the metallic sheet at the center of the TimeQuest 2 comic and said, "Wear bracelet." At once a thin gold rectangle detached itself, floated into the air, and wrapped tightly around my wrist. A small screen appeared on it, scrolling the words "Thank you for purchasing TimeQuest 2—ready to time-travel." A rash of goose bumps traveled from my neck to my feet as I remembered our dangerous quest for the *Superman #1* comic. Would this new adventure put our lives at risk all over again?

"Wear bracelet," Paul said. Another gold rectangle tore away from the metallic sheet and wrapped around his wrist. He dumped the TimeQuest 2 comic into his backpack and zipped it up. "The *Titanic* sets sail from Southampton, England, on April 10, 1912, and sinks in the North Atlantic on April 14 after hitting an iceberg. So we have to pick a time between those two days."

"Bracelet, transport us to the morning of April 13, 1912, on board the *Titanic* steamship!" I commanded.

"Preparing to warp the space-time continuum," the bracelets announced as they glowed brightly. My skin felt warm and tingly, and then a dizzy feeling overcame me. I held my stomach and suddenly regretted eating a

crusty purple french fry from the year 100,000. Paul looked like he was going to puke, and then everything went black.

We Meet Sean

We appeared on a giant ship's deck sitting on an uncomfortable iron bench with fancy armrests. Around us, metal cables extended up to a towering flagpole and then branched into a complicated web fit for a mutant spider. I jumped to my feet, rubbed my eyes to make sure it wasn't a dream, and then ran over to the white metal railing to get a better look. Down the length of the ship, four huge funnels stretched skyward at slight angles—they were yellow with black tips, as if sky-high, chocolate-dipped Twinkies had fallen from the stars and smashed into the boat.

"It worked!" I shouted. "We're on the *Titanic*!" As the huge boat cut through the ocean, mounds of water sped away from the hull and broke into small waves. The ship didn't rock one bit as we cruised toward a perfect horizon. Three of the massive funnels released puffs of black smoke that mingled together and trailed into the distance.

"Good timing," Paul said, glancing at his TimeQuest bracelet. "It's April 13, 1912, at 11:30 A.M. We're heading across the ocean for New York!" A misty sea breeze drenched my legs. I should have worn long pants. But I have very bad luck while wearing jeans, so I usually wear shorts all year round. Mom complains about it all the time.

All around us, adults sat in antique wooden deck chairs sipping drinks while children ran around playing with tops or blowing whistles. Oddly, every single person wore a hat, even the kids. I wasn't sure if I even owned a hat, and it made me certain that I had done a terrible packing job.

"I tell you, this ship is unsinkable," a man with a brass cane said, walking behind us. "She's the eighth wonder of the world."

"Even Zeus himself couldn't down her with his largest lightning bolt," another added.

"I kinda feel bad for these people," I whispered. "How much time do we have to find Sean and get the baseball card before this ship sinks?"

"According to *The Titanic Disaster for Dummies*, the ship hits the iceberg at 11:40 tomorrow night—that gives us about thirty-six hours to find Sean and get the card." Paul leaned over the railing and flipped through a bright yellow book. The passersby gave him a curious look and then continued walking.

"Are you crazy!" I said, grabbing the book from

Paul. "We don't want to attract attention to ourselves."
I tossed the book overboard, but a wind blew it back to
the ship, and it crashed against cables and steel girders
on the way down.

"It doesn't matter. I already read the whole thing.
C'mon, I'll show you around." Paul took me on a tour
of the entire boat. It had a gym filled with antique
bicycles and rowing machines, a pool filled with ocean
water, fancy dining rooms and lounges, libraries,
squash courts, miniature golf, massage parlors, eleva-
tors, and long decks that girls walked across very slowly
while carrying umbrellas. Everywhere we went all the
people talked about was how amazing the ship was, but
I wasn't impressed.

"A Disney cruise my parents took me on was better,"
I said as we entered a first-class restaurant called Café
Parisienne. Small wicker tables stood between potted
palm trees. Fancy wooden paneling covered the walls
and ceiling, and large windows overlooked the ocean.

"C'mon. It's good for 1912!" Paul argued. "You're
disrespecting the *Titanic*?"

"You must be in third class, young lads," a woman
sitting at a small circular table said. She looked older
than my dad, even though she had a wildly tangled
head of black hair. A thick woolen shawl covered
with dust and cobwebs was wrapped around her. She
stared fixedly at a small beaker filled with red liquid
that sat amid a clutter of chemical bottles and strange

laboratory equipment. "My analysis is complete—the yogurt on this ship does contain real fruit!"

"Uh, actually we're in fourth class," I said nervously, hoping not to give away our true identity.

"You have a marvelous sense of humor. I am Dr. Alice Grim, personal physician. House calls are my specialty." She packed the chemicals and glass tubes away in a small black bag and pushed it under the table. Two deckhands appeared and placed a large wooden screen in front of the window by Dr. Grim's table.

"I can't have harsh sunlight interfering with my experiments—thank you, gents," Dr. Grim said, giving each one a gold coin with strange writing on it.

"Our pleasure, Dr. Grim."

"You have a cool name for a doctor," Paul observed.

"Cool? How can a name be hot or cold?"

"Uh, nice, I meant to say *nice* name."

"Speaking of such, is one of you named Sean?" Dr. Grim checked the time on a shiny gold pocket watch connected to a chain, then took a sip from a tiny glass containing brown liquid and an olive. Her eyes opened wide, and she poured the rest of it into her black bag, causing a small puff of steam to rise up and float away. "Later we will see if that olive is Mediterranean in origin."

"We're looking for Sean, too!" Paul answered excitedly.

"I have arranged to be his attending doctor during the journey to New York. Apparently, he has a rare case of Miasma Corrosus, which greatly intrigues me. I must perform some tests. Are you his brothers?"

"Yes!" Paul blurted.

"No," I said, frowning at Paul.

"Well, which is it?" Dr. Grim said. She smiled, showing off two gold teeth that glinted brightly.

Actually, we're from the future, and we came to steal Sean's baseball card before this ship sinks, I imagined myself saying. I already felt guilty about what we were planning to do, but I felt even worse about wrecking Dad's most prized possession. I still couldn't bear to tell the whole truth.

"*I'm* Sean's brother," Paul explained. "But Brian here is his second cousin twice removed. He was almost removed a third time but he fought back."

I slapped my forehead and hung my head in embarrassment.

"How droll!" Dr. Grim said, slapping her knee. "I would be honored if you two would join me for dinner tonight. I'm sure the fare here is much better than in steerage."

"Well, I guess we'll come, if they'll let us," I said, trying to sound innocent. After all, we weren't really third class, fourth class, or any class. We were trespassers! What if she found out? Maybe she wasn't really a doctor after all but a werewolf hired by the ship's owners to sniff out stowaways. Her name and those gold fangs gave me the chills. "Thanks for inviting us, Dr. *Grim.*"

Just then a thin boy with short black hair limped into the restaurant. With one hand he held onto a white-haired woman wearing thick purple glasses. In the other he held a small metal box.

"That's gotta be Sean," I whispered to Paul, elbowing him. "I bet the baseball card is in that metal thing he's carrying."

"Then let's just grab it and warp home," Paul suggested. Dr. Grim eyed us curiously.

"No way, that's too evil. We should at least ask him for it."

"Mother, I require vanilla ice cream with three ounces of chocolate syrup," the boy said, approaching our table.

"After your visit with the doctor, dear," the woman said. "I want to see that you're well taken care of during the voyage."

"Who's she?" Paul whispered.

"That's Mattie's grandmother, Esmerelda, and my great-great-grandmother. She bought the Honus Wagner card originally."

"Ah, you must be Esmerelda," the doctor said, standing up. "We exchanged telegrams. Dr. Alice Grim, at your service." She opened a small gold box, took out a business card, and handed it to the boy's mother.

"So nice to meet you," Esmerelda said, placing the card in a purple purse. "It's positively noble of you to agree to attend to my delicate Sean. Now if you'll

excuse me, I must see some acquaintances in the ladies' lounge. Sean, be nice to the doctor, and I'll purchase that ice cream when I return."

"Yes, Mother." Sean let his mother kiss him on the cheek, and then she left the room. "You don't look at all like a doctor," Sean said to Dr. Grim. "Doctors are supposed to have white hair and wear spectacles."

"Looks can be deceiving, lad. Take your relations here, for example. I never would have guessed that they were your brother and cousin." Dr. Grim untangled a knot in her hair with a fork, allowing a spider to escape and scurry away.

Sean turned to me and Paul and narrowed his eyes suspiciously. My heart started pounding. "Um, we have to go shovel coal," I said, pulling Paul away. "Fourth-class passengers have duties, y'know." We walked quickly out of the restaurant and slammed the door behind us.

"Well, that went pretty well," Paul observed.

"Now Sean'll never give us that card," I moaned. "Our secret's out already!"

"At least we know what we're doing for dinner."

Dejected, we meandered into a room that was brightly lit by a massive glass dome in the ceiling. Beneath the dome, two big staircases curved together, joined by a shiny wooden banister. An intricately carved clock held by two angels overlooked the top of the stairs, and a brass boy held a torch at the bottom. Elegant tiles covered the landing below, where a man in a fancy uniform crawled around looking for something. He had a white mustache and beard, and he wore a red cap with gold leaves, a flag, and a bright white star on it.

"Blasted button," he mumbled.

"That's Edward John Smith," Paul whispered. "His picture was in that book you threw overboard. "He's the *Titanic*'s captain!"

Suddenly, I spotted a shiny brass button at the bottom of the staircase between two pillars. I snatched it up and gave it to Captain Smith.

"Imagine that," the captain said, gently removing the button from my hand. "I'm positively overwhelmed with gratitude. I insist that you two join me on the bridge before we reach New York. I'll give you a complete tour of the inner workings of this ship." He glanced at a gold pocket watch connected to a chain. "Oh, dear, I'm late." He patted me and Paul on the head, put the button in his pocket, and wandered off.

"Well, at least we're good at making friends on this boat," I said, sitting at the bottom of the stairs. Paul sat next to me, and we watched the passengers walk by for a while. Paul pointed out everybody that he recognized from reading that book.

Eventually, Sean appeared at the top of the staircase, staring down at us with an evil glare. Then he *ran* down the stairs toward us, clutching the metal box in his right hand and a bowl of ice cream in his left.

We Try to Get the Baseball Card

"Hey, what happened to your limp?" I asked Sean as he leaped onto the banister and slid down next to Paul. He sat next to us on the bottom step, placed the metal box on the steps, and dug into his ice cream with a silver spoon.

"I only limp when I want something."

"But what about your Miasma Corrosus?" Paul asked.

"I made that up," Sean said. "I got tricky smarts." He pointed to his head.

"You mean you've been lying about it your whole life?" I blurted. "And it's totally fake, like cooties?"

"Hmm, cooties?" Sean asked, rubbing his chin.

"Never mind," Paul said.

"Why'd you tell Dr. Grim that you're my relations? You're pretty bad liars, not like me."

"We're baseball card collectors," Paul said. "We've been trying to find you." Sean scratched his head and looked at us in confusion.

"See, we want to buy the baseball card that you're carrying in that box," I added.

Sean looked at us with wide eyes. "You're spies? Who sent you? My brother? He's still envious that *he* didn't get the card with Honus Wagner's signature."

"No, we work for ourselves," Paul replied. "But we'll give you five dollars for that baseball card." He pulled the bag of antique money out of his backpack.

"How could a nickel-pack card be worth five dollars?" Sean asked. He popped open the box, revealing the bright orange Honus Wagner card. Just as Mattie's diary had said, the card was in perfect condition, as shiny as the day it was printed. Honus's slick black hair was parted down the middle, and his gray jersey was buttoned tightly against his neck—which probably explained the glum look on his face. Or maybe he was just concerned that I might bite his head off. His handwritten signature stretched across the bottom, covering one of the white buttons on his uniform.

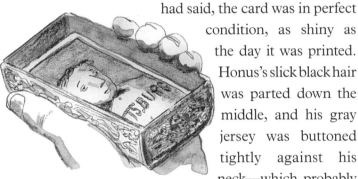

"We're from the future," I said, determined to tell the truth. "That baseball card will be worth a million dollars in our time." A lady wearing a raccoon around her neck walked by and gave me a funny look.

"You must be joking! You're hopeless liars."

"Fine, we'll give you fifteen dollars, but that's our final offer." Paul held out three wrinkled antique bills.

Sean grabbed the bills and stuffed them in his pocket. "I'll give you the card tomorrow." He handed me his empty ice-cream bowl, snapped the box shut, and ran upstairs.

"It might be too late then," I said, looking at Paul, who was still holding out his money hand. "We have only thirty hours left."

That evening we had dinner with Dr. Grim, Esmerelda, and Sean in the first-class dining room. Esmerelda wore a purple dress with sparkling beads on it, and Dr. Grim wore a white dinner suit. For some reason she still had that cobwebby shawl wrapped around her shoulders. It was easy to forget that we were on a ship—men wearing tuxedos milled around, delivering plates of gourmet food to passengers. The waiters gave me and Paul strange looks. Sean snickered at me when the waiter picked up my napkin and tucked it into my shirt collar.

"Why does your watch have only numbers on it?" Sean asked Paul. "Where are the clock hands?"

"In the future, watches tell time with no hands," Paul whispered back. He grinned nervously at Dr. Grim and Esmerelda and then moved his watch arm under the table.

"That's John Jacob Astor sitting over there," Dr. Grim said, gesturing toward a man with a black mustache. "He's one of the wealthiest men in America, worth over a hundred million dollars."

"Who needs millions when I have such lovely children," Esmerelda retorted. She licked her finger and fixed Sean's hair. He pushed her arm away.

"What hides inside that metal box you've been carrying around?" Dr. Grim asked Sean. "I'm sure we've all been curious."

"It's Honus Wagner, only the finest baseball player that ever lived," Sean answered, popping open the tin. "He got 158 hits last year!" I hoped Sean wouldn't hold the card in his dirty hands. That would lower its value by hundreds of thousands of dollars! Paul glanced at me nervously.

"American boys and their baseball card obsession," Dr. Grim remarked, extracting a pit out of an olive with her sharp golden tooth. "Where I'm from in England, we play—"

"I might sell it for fifteen dollars," Sean interrupted as he poured all the vegetables from his plate onto a napkin, folded it up, and buried it in the potted plant next to the table.

"Fifteen dollars!" Esmerelda shrieked. "That's an enormous sum for a baseball card."

"Pass it over here, if you don't mind, lad. I'd like to get a better look," Dr. Grim said. She licked some sauce off her fingers, pushed her dusty, soot-covered shawl away from her arms, and reached for the metal box.

"Well, Sean, don't be rude," Esmerelda said. "Dr. Grim would like to see your baseball card."

"Do something," I whispered to Paul as Sean reluctantly slid the box toward Dr. Grim. "She'll get the card dirty." Dr. Grim placed a round brass lens in her eye. Without touching the baseball card, she examined it carefully, muttering to herself. Then she reached below the table and fumbled around in her bagful of supplies. I so wished I had put the card in the plastic case we brought along—a few more seconds and it might be too late!

"The paint on this card may contain lead," Dr. Grim speculated. "Lead exposure would certainly not be beneficial to such a sickly boy, especially if he were to eat it. Surely you wouldn't mind if I took a paint sample?"

"I'd have to be a pretty stupid kid to eat a baseball card!" Sean shrieked. Esmerelda looked at him in shock. I suddenly wondered if all my bad dreams were the result of lead poisoning.

Dr. Grim retrieved a razor-sharp instrument from her bag. She leaned over the mint-condition baseball card and put the point near the orange background next to Honus Wagner's picture. Paul looked at me in a panic—Dr. Grim was about to ruin a million-dollar card! My palms started sweating as I tried to think of some way to distract her. I pictured Dad giving me advice: *Quick, grab the card and swallow it. Then she'll never get the paint sample she wants, muahahaha.*

"Don't touch my card," Sean ordered, scowling at her.

"Dear, how can you say such a thing?" Esmerelda scolded. Paul grabbed a pepper shaker and began sniffing it.

"Aw, Mother."

Just as Dr. Grim was about to stab the baseball card, Paul released a humongous sneeze—WAAAAHBLOOCH!—and fell off his chair, grabbing the end of the tablecloth on the way down. A tremendous crash of metal and broken china caused everyone in the room to look over at us. The metal box slid across the table, where Sean snatched it up. He quickly snapped the cover back onto it.

"Sorry, I'm allergic to broccoli," Paul said weakly, smiling at me. I nodded at him approvingly. Close call. Sean's card was still untouched and in perfect condition, although Paul was covered in peas and brown gooey sauce.

"I'm allergic to *all* vegetables," Sean said, reaching under the table.

"Good work," I whispered when Paul limped back to his chair. Esmerelda unfolded a paper fan and waved it quickly. With a bright red face, she looked around at all the tables and smiled nervously.

"Don't panic," Paul whispered to me after things had settled down, "but now I can't find my backpack." I looked down at the floor where it should have been, but I saw only scraps that had fallen off the table.

"Is this all you packed for the whole voyage?" Sean asked, sifting through Paul's backpack on the other side of the table.

"Hey, give that back!" Paul demanded.

"Sean, that doesn't belong to you!" Esmerelda said.

"What's this?" Sean pulled a DVD out of the pack. It was *Titanic*—the movie!

"You packed that?" I asked, looking at Paul in disbelief. He shrugged.

"'Leonardo DiCaprio and Kate Winslet light up the screen as Jack and Rose, the young friends who find one another on the maiden voyage of the 'unsinkable' RMS *Titanic*,'" Sean read from the back of the DVD case. "'But when the doomed luxury liner collides with an iceberg in the frigid North Atlantic, their friendship becomes a thrilling race for survival. The 1997 James Cameron film won eleven Academy Awards, including Best Picture.'" Sean looked at me and Paul with wide eyes.

Sean popped open the DVD case, revealing the shiny silver disk. Confused, he gazed at his reflection in it.

"You must excuse Sean," Esmerelda said, grabbing the DVD and backpack and handing them back to Paul. "He's quite weary from traveling. So, what a delightful evening! We must do this again sometime." She fanned herself really fast.

Sean stared at me and Paul with a dazed look for a while. Then he opened the metal box and stared at the Honus Wagner card.

Later that evening, Sean led us back to his luxury suite. Through the hallway window I noticed that the *Titanic* sped toward a wispy orange sunset at the horizon—a glowing streak blazed across the ocean surface, lighting up an ocean-long highway for the ship to travel down. We had only one more sunset to go before that path would lead to a terrible nightmare. I wondered if Paul and I could do something about that.

"Are you two Martians?" Sean asked. "You must use that watch with no clock hands to communicate with your flying ship. I bet it takes a long time to get here from Mars."

"Nope, we warped right onto the ship using our time-travel bracelets," I corrected. I lifted up my sleeve and showed Sean the shiny bracelet, which flashed all sorts of strange symbols.

"So you *are* from the future?"

"We told you," Paul said.

"That thing in your backpack was real? You know that this ship's going to sink? But that's impossible."

Sean opened the door to his cabin, pulled us in,

and then slammed it shut. The room was a first-class stateroom. "You can stay in the servants' room if you want. But you have to tell me everything that's going to happen—the whole truth!"

We sat at a fancy table under a stained-glass chandelier and told Sean the entire story—about Dad's wrecked baseball card, the TimeQuest comic, and especially about the fate of the most famous luxury liner in the world.

"But everyone says this ship is unsinkable. How does it happen?" Sean asked in bewilderment as he stared at the shiny silver cover of the TimeQuest 2 comic.

"A big iceberg," Paul answered.

"But they said that watertight compartments down

below could hold the ocean even if we hit an iceberg. Four of them could fill up, and we'd still be afloat."

"The *Titanic* won't hit the iceberg head on," Paul explained. "It'll scrape along the side and make a gash across six of those compartments. They'll fill up and tilt the boat headfirst into the water. Then it'll crack in half and sink to the bottom. The boat won't be found again until 1985."

"What? Will anybody survive?"

"Less than half the people."

"We have to do something!" Sean screamed. "We'll tell Captain Smith, he'll know what to do!"

"Uh, that wasn't part of our original plan," Paul mumbled.

"So you were just going to take my baseball card and leave me to drown?" Sean accused.

Paul and I drooped our heads and didn't say anything for a while. That little guilty whisper inside my brain suddenly exploded into a sickening scream. We had been so busy planning how we were going to get the baseball card that we never stopped to think about all the people on board the *Titanic* or what we might be able to do to help them. Sean was right—taking the Honus Wagner card and leaving now would be selfish and cruel. No matter how much we were afraid of messing up the space-time continuum, it was our responsibility to prevent this ship from sinking. I guess it didn't matter very much that Paul ate all the grax.

We Devise a Rescue Plan

That night we stayed up late in Sean's suite, planning how we could save the *Titanic*. I couldn't believe that we were going to mess around with the space-time continuum on purpose. What would Mr. O say? What about the butterfly effect? But then I thought about all those innocent people, and I focused on coming up with a good plan. Anyway, how could helping people possibly make the future worse?

"Look, the boat has toilets that actually flush!" Sean said, pulling a chain repeatedly as he stared at us with a big grin.

"Oh golly, oh gee, pinch me, I must be dreaming," Paul said in his most sarcastic, monotone voice.

"Nope, it's real," Sean retorted. "And look, this reading lamp has a dial that automatically adjusts the brightness. So we can read our rescue plans—after we make them, of course."

"OK, let's figure this out," I said. "The boat hits

the iceberg at 11:40 tomorrow night, so that gives us exactly twenty-four hours to do something."

Someone knocked at the door.

"That must be room service," Sean said, jumping out of his seat. He ran to the door and opened it. A man in a red cap rolled in a tray of ice cream and other desserts. Then he spooned out the ice cream into fancy blue bowls and covered each with toppings.

"Enjoy, young lads," he said, tipping his hat to us.

"Keep the change," Sean said, handing the man a five-dollar bill.

"Thank you kindly, that's very generous of you," the man said, pocketing the money. "Are you one of the Rockefeller boys?"

"Yeah, sure, if it pleases you," Sean said, gently pushing the man out the door. He slammed the door and ran back over to the ice cream.

"Can we get started already?" I asked impatiently.

Sean tucked a napkin into his shirt and dug away at his ice cream.

While Sean pigged out on dessert, I wrote out a list of all our rescue options. We had to think carefully because we didn't want to cause a huge panic, make things worse, or convince people that we were nuts.

Options for Saving the *Titanic*

A. Tell Captain Edward John Smith the truth: we're

from the future, and we know the ship's going to hit an iceberg and sink. (Brian's plan)

B. Sneak into the navigation room and turn the ship's wheel so the *Titanic* travels south, away from the cold waters of the North Atlantic and the icebergs. (Paul's plan)

C. Sneak down to the boiler room and empty a pouch of marbles onto the floor next to the giant coal-eating boilers. The men shoveling the coal will slip and fall, get bumps on their heads, and have to go to the ship's doctor to get bandages. When they're gone, sneak over to the boilers and shut them down, making the ship stop. (Sean's plan)

"But what happens when the men come back?" I asked Sean. "Won't they turn everything back on again?"

"While they're gone we steal all the coal," Sean finished.

"There's five thousand tons of it!" I argued.

"Then we'll just bust things up down there until something breaks. It'll be fun."

"I got it!" Paul blurted, snapping his fingers. "We'll show Captain Smith the *Titanic* movie! The ship sinks in the movie exactly like it happens in real life. That'll convince him of the truth!"

"Is that the shiny disk I found in your backpack during dinner?" Sean asked.

"Yep, watch," Paul said, plunking it into his portable

DVD player. Immediately, the movie began playing on the tiny screen.

"Wow, it's an un-silent picture," Sean observed. "Mother takes me to silent ones all the time. I just saw *Dr. Jekyll and Mr. Hyde* before this trip. It cost a nickel."

"Going to the movies costs ten dollars in our time," I added.

"How droll," Sean sneered. "I can make up jokes like that, too." He frowned at us.

We watched the movie for a while, but the love story made me and Paul fall asleep. When we woke up, light streamed in through the windows. Sean was in the exact same spot we left him, watching the movie—except now he was surrounded by empty bags of popcorn.

"You're still watching it?" Paul asked, rubbing his eyes groggily.

"I watched the whole thing three times!" Sean said excitedly. "I can't believe that poor guy fell in love with that snooty rich girl. Ugh! She's *so* obnoxious."

"It's 11 A.M.," Paul said, glancing at his watch. "It's April 14! Today's the day! Why didn't you wake us up? Now we have less than thirteen hours left." Paul tried to fix his messed-up hair in a gold-framed mirror, but a cowlick kept popping up.

"I lost track of time," Sean said, crumpling up a popcorn bag and tossing it on the floor. "I've been thinking—I want to keep my baseball card. Maybe

I can trade you something else—like this game." He picked up a wooden paddle with a ball connected to it. He paddled it wildly, grinning from ear to ear like he was having all the fun in the world.

"This thing is going overboard," Paul said, grabbing the paddle from Sean.

"I spent the rest of your money, so we must agree on a trade."

"You've spent fifteen dollars on 1912 snacks?" I said, picking up a crumpled popcorn bag. "It should have all cost a quarter!"

"I'm a good tipper. Anyway, you fellas said you spend piles of dough on the movie pictures all the time in the future." He yanked the paddle back from Paul.

"Yeah, but there's inflation, and—oh, who cares!" I hollered. "We have to find the captain. Let's go with plan A. Only the truth can save this ship."

"OK, but if it doesn't work, don't even think about taking my baseball card and warping back to the future," Sean threatened. "I hid your time-travel bracelets while you were sleeping. I'm not giving them back until you help me save the ship."

I quickly looked at my wrist—the bracelet was missing! Paul and I stared at each other.

Suddenly, the reality of our situation dawned on me. If we didn't succeed with our rescue plan, Paul and I would drown in the icy cold Atlantic along with everyone else.

It was like one of Dad's old bedtime stories, only

this one might not have such a happy ending. Was a baseball card really worth all the trouble? I tried to imagine the look on Dad's face when I handed him a Honus Wagner card that was even better than the one I had destroyed—but all I could see was a vivid image of the *Titanic* tilting into the ocean and swallowing up the helpless people.

"It doesn't feel so good to be doomed, does it?" Sean sneered. "Now you're in it just as deep as the rest of us."

"Give those back!" I whined. "We were gonna help anyway!"

"We'll see. Oh yeah, while you boys slept I read that funny paper you have," Sean said, adjusting his cap while Paul packed up the DVD player. "Which one of you drew that? It's swell."

I grabbed the TimeQuest 2 comic book out of Paul's backpack and opened it. The first few pages had filled in with cartoon drawings of me, Paul, and Sean! It showed me destroying Dad's baseball card, sending away for the TimeQuest 2 comic, the futuristic deliveryman coming to our house, me and Paul warping onto the *Titanic*, our dinner with Dr. Grim and Esmerelda, and our night of planning the rescue. One full-page drawing showed Paul pulling the tablecloth while Sean grabbed the box containing Honus Wagner. A bunch of chirping birds circled Paul's head while he lay on the floor. Another box showed a bright light bulb above me

when I finally realized that we had to do something to save this ship. A caption read "Will our three heroes save the *Titanic* before it sinks? Or will Sean just keep eating unhealthy snacks until the ship plunges into the icy cold North Atlantic? Read on to find out!"

"Hey, this comic says you're eating too much junk food," I remarked.

"Yeah, it doesn't like me," Sean said. "I tore the rest of those weird metal bracelets out of it last night and hid them too. The book started beeping and stuff until I put it back in Paul's bag. Good thing you fellas sleep like logs."

I flipped to the center of the comic and noticed that the extra time-travel bracelets were missing! I just hoped he hadn't thrown them all overboard—then even if we saved the *Titanic* we'd be stuck in 1912 permanently!

We Attempt a Daring Rescue

A few minutes later, we ran down a red-carpeted hall-way that led to the ship's bridge. Sean walked slowly, knocking on everybody's door on the way, and then ducking around a corner when people opened them. A bunch of passengers yelled at me and Paul, so we each grabbed one of Sean's hands and dragged him at the proper emergency speed.

"This way," Paul said.

We ignored a sign that read No Admittance—Staff Only and climbed a white circular staircase that took us into a bright room with giant windows overlooking the front of the ship—the main bridge. Antique radio equipment covered the walls, and six metal statues that looked like parking meters stood around the room—a big metal dial was attached to each one, with labels like Full Ahead, Dead Slow Ahead, Stand By, Stop, Half Astern, Full Astern. An enormous ship's wheel stood in the center of the room.

"Hey, you're not supposed to be in here," a man said.

"We need to speak to Captain Smith right away," I explained. "It's an emergency."

"It's against regulations for children to be on the bridge. I could lose my job."

"Here, this should change your mind," Sean said, reaching into Paul's backpack and grabbing the bag of antique money. He handed it to the man and crossed his arms confidently, tapping his foot on the carpet.

"Hey!" Paul blurted.

"You must be those kids that paid fifteen dollars for refreshments. My friend on kitchen duty told me about it. You're the Guggenheim kids or something, right?"

"If it pleases you," Sean said impatiently. "Where's the captain?"

"Captain Smith is currently in the men's lounge with some of the ship's builders," the man said, stuffing the money into his pocket.

"Only ten hours left," Paul said, eyeing his watch.

We raced down another hallway until we came to a stuffy room filled with men wearing fancy clothes. We spotted the fuzzy-bearded captain on a couch at the far end of the room and sprinted over to him.

"Captain Smith, we're those kids that found your button yesterday, remember?" I said quickly. "You said you'd take us on a tour of the bridge. Can we go now?"

"Take a good look at these fine young lads, every-body," Captain Smith said, gesturing toward us. "They will inherit our world some day, and none could be more deserving. The pinnacle of upbringing, I tell you." Everybody looked at me and Paul strangely.

"Can we go now, please?" I said.

"I'll tell you what," the captain began. "I have some meetings this afternoon, but I'll gladly give you a tour after my retirement party this evening. Thirty-two years with the White Star Line, you know."

"No, it might be too late by then," I interrupted. "The ship's gonna sink at 11:40 tonight!" The whole room suddenly became very quiet.

"Nonsense, this ship is a colossus," another man said. "It's unsinkable."

"A lot of superstition and fearful tidings have been circulating out from steerage," the captain said. "I assure you that none of them are true. Now run along and find me again at dinner."

"We're not leaving until you watch this DVD—it explains everything," Paul stated, placing the portable DVD player on the table in front of Captain Smith. He looked on curiously as Paul placed the movie in the DVD holder and hit "Play." At once, large white letters appeared on a blue background: "Battery low—recharge battery using included adapter." A small animation showed the DVD player being plugged into a device that attached to a wall outlet.

"Fascinating," Captain Smith said. "A small contraption that tells you what to do. I've never seen its equal. Are you John Jacob Astor's children? This must have cost a small fortune!"

"Sean!" Paul said angrily. "You played this all night and wasted the battery!"

"I did not!" Sean insisted. "Um, what's a 'battery'?"

"Please tell me you brought a recharger," I said to Paul.

He reached into his backpack and pulled out a small black device with a plug. "I told you I packed right," he said. "I can recharge the battery, but I don't have the wire that can play the DVD player directly from the wall outlet. It'll take seven hours to get enough juice to watch the movie."

We politely excused ourselves and ran back to Sean's stateroom. Paul yanked the table lamp's wire out of an outlet and immediately plugged the recharger into it. A small red light on it began blinking.

"Now what? It won't be ready until 8:30 tonight," I said. "That's cutting it too close."

"Let's go tell my mom about the ship sinking," Sean said. "She always believes everything I say. Last night, I told her you boys were stowaways discovered by the Master of Arms in a crate down in the storage hold. She said that I was a good person for helping wayward children less fortunate than me."

With no time to lose, we ran out the door, down another hallway, and into the ladies' lounge. Esmerelda sat on a violet couch, knitting a scarf. She wore a yellow dress that flowed all the way down to the floor. As soon as Sean entered the room, he began limping. He hobbled over to her, wheezing.

"Mother, Mother, this ship's going to sink. You have to do something about it right away," Sean whined. "The captain didn't believe us."

"Oh, Sean, you have such a vivid imagination," Esmerelda responded. She grabbed Sean and smothered him with a kiss while he fought to get away. "Dr. Grim is looking for you. She needs a small blood sample to help her formulate a Miasma Corrosus antidote.

Be a dear and take care of that now, please."

Suddenly, Dr. Grim, who had been sitting in a chair hidden behind a large fern, got up and approached us holding a hypodermic needle that was large enough to inject a dinosaur. She gripped it tightly with both hands and grinned, her sharp gold teeth glinting. Sean dropped his metal box and backed away from her until he tripped on a chair and fell.

Now was the perfect time to put the Honus Wagner card in the protective case that we had packed. I fell to my knees and pulled the Lucite case out of my pocket. After popping open the tin, with a bead of sweat dripping down my face, I lifted the delicate card by its edges and moved it closer to the protective holder. My hand was shaking so much that I couldn't slip the card into the narrow opening. Paul kneeled and grabbed my wrist. With his guiding hand, I carefully inserted the card into the small case, snapped it shut, and then placed it safely inside the metal box. Operation complete.

Dr. Grim wrapped her cobwebby shawl around her head, walked over to the windows, and shut all the curtains with one quick pull of a rope. She stepped slowly toward Sean. "Stay still, that's a good boy, this won't hurt a bit. I need only half a pint or so to run some tests back in my lab."

"Mother!" Sean yelled, scrambling behind the couch. "I'm not keen on needles!"

"A little pinch is all you'll feel," Dr. Grim reassured,

climbing over the couch to reach Sean. "And your mother promised to buy you ice cream afterward." The whites in her eyes seemed to glow red, and her messy hair looked like slithering snakes.

"Run!" Sean hollered. He kicked Dr. Grim in the knee.

Hopping on one foot, Dr. Grim fell onto Esmerelda's lap, where she was poked by her knitting needle. "Ow!" Dr. Grim screamed.

I grabbed Sean's box, and then we ran out the door and sprinted down the hallway, knocking over a maid carrying a pile of towels. I peeked over my shoulder, only to see Dr. Grim bolt into the hallway after us, gripping her needle tightly.

"You're being very naughty," she called out. "Your mother is paying me a great deal for my time."

"The elevator," I said, pointing to a tiny room protected by a gate of metal bars. After I pulled it open, we rushed in, and then Paul slid the gate shut just as Dr. Grim arrived. She shoved the hypodermic needle between the bars, but Sean slinked into the far corner, just out of reach.

"Really, dear, your disobedience is unfounded. I mean you no harm," she declared, trying repeatedly to stab Sean.

"Go away. Tell Mother I'm a fake. There is no Miasma Corrosus," Sean whined. "This is too much."

"Nonsense. I've already begun working on the antidote.

Other children with your same symptoms await a cure. Think of how this will benefit the world. Now *give me your blood!*"

I pressed a brass lever into the "down" position, sparking the elevator to life and forcing Dr. Grim to remove her arm. We slowly descended into the bowels of the ship. Soon the elevator couldn't go any farther, so we ran out and zigzagged through a maze of stairwells until we were safely tucked away in the *Titanic*'s belly. The groaning and hissing of steam engines came from all around us, mixed in with the yelling of men and the clanking of steel. A few rats scurried into dark corners. We finally stopped to rest in a cavernous room filled impossibly high with crates and canvas bags. My sneakers squeaked on the slimy, wet floor. (Note to self: wear boots next time you descend into the hold of the *Titanic*.)

"She'll never find us here," Paul said.

"She's a mad scientist," Sean whined. "I've read about them in books. She can use a smelling potion to track me down. I'll never be safe."

"You're with me and Brian," Paul assured him. "We've handled stuff like this before."

While the ship's steam engines roared and clanked somewhere nearby, we walked through the huge cargo hold, looking at the labels on each big crate. For dozens of companies, the *Titanic* was carrying an amazing amount of stuff across the Atlantic: cheese, shelled walnuts, potatoes, refrigerators, tennis balls, an antique

car, rare books, dirt, feathers, rabbit hair, leather, gum, and cans of dragon's blood.

"Dragon's blood, what's that?" Sean asked. I shrugged my shoulders.

Paul climbed up and lifted the lid of the crate, which was labeled "Brown Brothers and Company—76 Cases Dragon's Blood, 3 Cases Gum." Then he pulled out a small, shiny tin can and read the label on it.

"'Dragon's blood—a red liquid obtained from various plants of the agave family. The early Greeks and Romans believed that it had medicinal properties. Currently used primarily as a varnish on violins. Store at room temperature.'"

A metal door slammed at the far end of the cargo hold. A shadowy figure slowly approached us. We stood perfectly still, too terrified to move.

"Sean, are you down here?" Dr. Grim's voice called out in a sickly sweet tone. "Why don't you show yourself, there's a good lad."

"Sean, get in the crate, I have an idea," I whispered, helping him into the big box. "Hide in the far back." Sean climbed up and disappeared into the crate. Then Paul slammed it shut and sat on top of it.

I knocked on the back of the crate and whispered to him through an open knot in the wood. "Sean, when I give the signal, cry out in pain."

"OK," Sean said faintly from inside the crate. "I hope you fellas know what you're doing."

Dr. Grim's footsteps became louder, until she calmly walked out of the darkness and stood next to us.

"We trapped Sean for you," I said to Dr. Grim. "He's inside the box."

"What!" Sean called out from within the crate. "You betrayed me! I'll get you for this! You pretended to be my friends and then gave me over to the enemy. I'll never give you back those bracelets now! How could you? People from the future are horrible! I hope this ship sinks just so you go down with it!"

"Excellent work, lads," Dr. Grim said, smiling. "A simple blood sample is all I need." Sweat dripped from her frazzled hair and rolled down her cheek.

"Stab him with that needle right through the crate," I whispered to Dr. Grim. "He's hiding right at the front of it."

"Brilliant idea," she said, quickly slamming the business end of her giant needle through the side of the big box. Then she pulled on the big rubber plunger. The glass tube began filling with a red liquid.

I ran around to the back of the crate and whispered to Sean, "Start screaming in pain. Now!"

"Oh ... I get it," Sean said. He started yelling. "Ow! Ow! You stabbed me! You're such an evil mad scientist! Ohhhh, I'm feeling faint."

Dr. Grim murmured softly until the big needle was full of blood—dragon's blood, and our trick went off perfectly. A few minutes later, Dr. Grim rapped on the

big crate and thanked Sean for his time. Then she turned to me and Paul with glowing red eyes. The air in the cargo hold went cold, and I got goose bumps on my neck. A horrible stench of decay filled the air—or was that just dragon's blood? Paul and I backed away from Dr. Grim as a big grin stretched across her face.

"When was the last time you two gave blood?" she asked in a guttural tone. She reminded me a lot of my doctor back home.

"Who's there?" a man's voice asked from the shadows. "Nobody's allowed in here." Dr. Grim turned her head in surprise, pulled the cobwebby shawl up to her face, and then slinked into the shadows and disappeared. Quickly, we climbed into the crate and hid next to Sean until the guard was gone.

"Thanks," Sean whispered. "You chaps are experts. Sorry about those awful things I said."

Sean insisted that we hang out in the cargo hold for the rest of the day, until it was time to put our final plan into action. After all, Dr. Grim might come after him with an even bigger needle when she found out the truth. So we moved into the antique car and ate cheese and chocolates while we planned our revised strategy to save the *Titanic*.

Iceberg!

At 8:10 P.M. on Sunday, April 14, 1912, we put our final plan into action. I carried out my part by finding Captain Smith in the men's lounge. I casually walked up to him and smiled, wondering if he had already forgotten who I was. He glanced at me briefly and then went back to chatting with a bunch of important-looking people. Paul had told me what to say, so I took a deep breath and let it all out as best I could remember.

"Captain, there's no moon for visibility, and the ocean's too calm to see waves washing up against the icebergs. Haven't you been getting iceberg warnings all day from nearby ships? There are only enough lifeboats for half the people on board. The watertight doors don't go all the way to the ceiling. Everybody knows you're a really good captain, but you have to be a little more worried tonight."

"Ah, it's you, lad," the captain began, looking at me anxiously. "I did promise you a ship's tour. However, my retirement reception is running longer than expected, and I mustn't be rude. Run along, and I'll give you the tour tomorrow."

"Is that true, E.J.?" one of the men asked the captain. "Lifeboats for half on board?" The room went quiet, and everybody stared at the captain.

The captain didn't say anything. Instead, he took a small piece of paper out of his pocket that read "Greek steamer *Athenia* reports passing icebergs and large quantities of field ice today in latitude 41° 51′ N, longitude 49° 52′ W. Wish you and *Titanic* all success."

"I'll let Thomas Andrews explain," the captain replied nervously, placing the piece of paper back into his pocket. He gestured to a man with a big forehead and neatly combed hair. "He designed this ship."

"Well, a great deal of thought went into how many lifeboats we put on board," Thomas Andrews began, "and I am pleased to announce that the number of lifeboats on our glorious *Titanic* greatly exceeds Board of Trade Regulations for British vessels." Everybody cheered and went back to laughing and chattering.

"We figured you were going to react this way," I interrupted, leaning over and clutching two buttons on the captain's coat. I yanked them off and ran.

"What the devil! Unhand those! They're solid brass!"

"You'll have to catch me first." My heart racing, I sprinted out of the room and down the hallway, right up to Sean, who opened the door to a laundry closet. I ducked into the dark room, where Paul waited to hit "Play" on his portable DVD player. Sean slammed the door behind me.

"He went in there, mister," I heard Sean say from outside the closet. Moments later, the door opened again, and Captain Smith came running in.

"Now!" I commanded. Paul hit the "Play" button on the DVD player, I threw the brass buttons at Captain Smith, and we ran out of the room, slamming the door behind us. Sean, Paul, and I leaned against the door with all our might so the captain couldn't get out.

"What is the meaning of this!" Captain Smith yelled from inside the closet, banging on the door. "Somebody get the Master of Arms!" Suddenly, the movie's music started playing and the captain became quiet. Two gentlemen in tuxedos ran down the hallway and approached us warily.

"What prank is this?" Thomas Andrews said. "What have you done to the captain?"

"You boys should be spanked for your impudence!" the other added.

"It's no big deal, the captain's watching a movie," Paul said. He cracked the door open, and everybody peered into the dark closet, where Captain Smith was staring in awe at the tiny DVD screen.

"It's your ship, Andrews, exactly as you designed it, in a talking picture show!" the captain said. "You and

Ismay ought to come in and watch." Both men entered the closet, and we shut the door behind them.

"Time check," I said to Paul.

"8:20 P.M., exactly three hours and twenty minutes until the iceberg impact."

"The movie lasts three hours and fourteen minutes—I hope they won't have to watch the whole thing to get the idea," I said.

We sat in front of the door, eagerly listening to the men rant and rave about the movie—what the producers got right and parts that were inaccurate. "Look how fat they made you, E.J.," one of the men commented. "Andrews, you look like a true gentleman in the picture." All three of them gasped at the moment when the ship scraped up against the big iceberg, cutting a hole in its side that began filling the lower compartments with water.

At exactly 11:34 P.M., the closet door burst open, and all three men ran out into the hallway.

"I can't believe that fine girl fell in love with that poor ruffian," Thomas Andrews remarked. "Ugh, he was so obnoxious."

"You got that backward, mister," Sean argued.

"Never mind that," Captain Smith ordered. "To the bridge at once!" We all ran down the hallway, up the white staircase, and into the navigation room, where three officers looked out the giant bay window at a calm black sea.

"Murdoch, Moody, Hitchens, anything to report?" the captain asked frantically.

"Captain, you'll be wanting to see this," Officer Murdoch said, showing him the bright yellow book entitled *The Titanic Disaster for Dummies.* "A girl from steerage found it jammed between two girders on B deck."

"What witchcraft has overtaken my ship?" Captain Smith asked, flipping through the book.

"That's mine," Paul said, grabbing a pair of binoculars out of his backpack. "You better use these; the ones in the lookout tower are missing." He handed them to Captain Smith, who peered through them at the calm sea ahead of the ship. Carefully, he focused the binoculars and scanned the black horizon.

"Oh, my heavens," the captain muttered after a few minutes, gazing at a particular spot in the distance. "An iceberg, right ahead. Hard-a-starboard. Hard-a-starboard! Now!" he commanded. The man named Hitchens began turning the giant wheel frantically. "Murdoch, telegraph full a-stern to Bill in engineering. We need to slow down."

"No!" Paul protested. "Slowing down will make the ship turn slower also. Murdoch, don't do it!"

"I'm the captain here, lad!" Smith said angrily. Deep wrinkles appeared in his forehead, masking his usually cheerful appearance. Murdoch ran over to the silver telegraph machine—one of those statues that looked like a parking meter—clutched the handle, and looked back and forth between Paul and Captain Smith, bewildered.

"No," Thomas Andrews said. "Maintain speed. The boy's right. If we reverse engines, the rudders will become useless."

A bell rang out three times above us, and then a buzzer went off. The man named Moody picked up a receiver.

"That's the iceberg warning from the lookout tower!" Paul cried. "But we spotted it before them—we have a chance!" Maybe we had a chance, but I would have felt a lot better if I had known where our TimeQuest bracelets were.

"There it is!" Sean yelled, pointing out the window. Up ahead, a dim triangular mass appeared out of the blackness—the fateful iceberg that was supposed to sink the *Titanic*! It sat quietly in the water, waiting, as if it had no clue it would become the most famous iceberg in history.

But not if Paul could help it.

"Did you push her hard-a-starboard?" Captain Smith asked as Hitchens frantically turned the steering wheel.

"Don't you mean *turn left*?" Paul cried. "Left! Why can't you guys just say what you mean?" I had never seen Paul so hyper. He pushed Hitchens away from the ship's wheel and took control himself, turning the big wheel around and around.

While the *Titanic* sped straight for the iceberg, all the men stood silently as Paul frantically worked the controls. Moments later the iceberg was upon us—a giant frozen mountain as tall as the ship's deck. At first it seemed like we would hit it head on, but seconds later the ship's bow turned left, and then more left, and then further left, until the iceberg was off to our right. We passed by it *without* hearing any scraping, cutting, or ripping noise spelling the *Titanic*'s doom. Then Paul slammed the wheel in the opposite direction so the rear of the ship would swing away from the iceberg. We whizzed past the frozen monster without even a tiny jolt. As quickly as the iceberg had appeared, it disappeared behind us into the chilly night.

"Good work, young chap!" Andrews cried. Murdoch patted Paul on the back.

"That was a blue berg," the captain said, dabbing his forehead with a cloth. "It was recently overturned and covered with seawater. Those are awfully difficult to spot in time—good thing these magical boys can somehow divine the future. Our hull must have missed that by a good foot or so." Everybody stared at Sean, Paul, and me in awe.

"Aw, it was nothing," Sean said. "Just another heroic day's work for us." He ran over, pushed Paul out of the way, and strained to turn the big wheel.

Over the next few days, Sean, Paul, and I were treated like freakish, superpowered heroes. There was a big meeting during which we were asked all sorts of questions about our powers—and our stuff was laid out on the table: the DVD player, the *Titanic* movie, the TimeQuest 2 comic book, and *The Titanic Disaster for Dummies* book. We were swamped with questions by managers of the White Star Line, and I answered them all truthfully. Sean refused to talk unless they brought him vanilla pudding and pastries.

News of the dramatic near-miss was radioed ahead to New York, so when we got there on Wednesday morning, swarms of reporters were waiting at the dock to greet us. A marching band played "The Star Spangled Banner" to celebrate this historic moment—the largest ship in the world arriving in America. As the *Titanic* docked under the old-fashioned New York skyline, Paul and I sat on the same bench where we had first appeared and discussed our next move.

"Here," Sean said, running up to us and dumping four TimeQuest bracelets into my lap. "You kept up your end of the bargain. You can have this too, I guess." He handed me the Honus Wagner card, still safe and in mint condition inside the plastic case.

"Thanks, this will really make my dad happy," I said, grabbing it. I gave it a big kiss and then zipped it safely into a special pouch in Paul's backpack. Finally, after nine years of bad dreams and sadness, I could make Dad forgive me for eating his most prized possession. Even if he didn't ever tell me another treasure chest story, it would still be worth it.

"Bye, Sean," I said. "Thanks for all the help."

A loud cheer came from the dock as the first passengers disembarked from the *Titanic*. Reporters rushed to get on the boat but were held back by the ship's officers. Before the mobs onshore could get to us, Paul and I both said "Home" into our TimeQuest bracelets. Everything turned dark and hazy, and then ...

We Make a Shocking Discovery

Paul and I appeared in midair, and then we plunged into a free fall until we splashed into a small, oddly shaped lake filled with black liquid. I swam to the surface and took a deep breath, inhaling a horrible stench like rotting potatoes mixed with cough medicine. Floundering through the muck, I wondered if this swamp was anywhere near my house—I didn't remember it at all. Suddenly, Sean splashed on top of us!

"Help!" he cried, flopping around in the smelly water. "I can't swim!"

We dragged Sean to shore and collapsed onto a pebbly beach. Out of breath, I flopped onto my back and looked up at the hazy orange sky. The rocks dug into my skin like knives.

"How did you get here?" Paul asked.

"I didn't give back *all* of your TimeQuest bracelets," Sean replied. "I told you, I got tricky smarts. I said

'Home' into the bracelet, just like you, so I could see what the future was like."

I remembered the TimeQuest comic's instructions: *once you visit a time period, you may not return to any date within fifty years of that period using your TimeQuest bracelets, but you may always travel home.*

"Now Sean's stuck with us," I whispered to Paul. "We can't go back to 1912, and these bracelets are programmed with a home time of 2002. There's no changing that!"

"So this is what the future looks like, huh?" Sean remarked. "Where are all the houses?"

I looked around. We weren't home at all—there were no people or buildings anywhere—only lots of small lakes filled with black water like the one we had landed in. That's when I noticed something terrible: the pebbles on the beach weren't rocks at all. They were tiny bits of man-made things, like plates, silverware, toys, paper, concrete, and lots of other stuff. I quickly looked at my flashing TimeQuest bracelet. The display read "Warped to HOME—Earth era: 2002. Butterfly-effect changes in effect."

"We've changed things!" I cried, looking at Paul in horror. "Saving the *Titanic* has somehow mashed up all the houses here into tiny little pebbles and made all these lakes!"

"Wait a minute," Paul responded, running to the top

of a small hill. "Those aren't lakes! They're ... They're ... footprints!"

"What!" I sprang to my feet and darted up to Paul. Sure enough, tremendous paw prints with seven clawed toes dotted the landscape all the way to the horizon. Each one was filled with that smelly black liquid.

I wouldn't be able to give Dad the Honus Wagner card because he wasn't home anymore. A sinking feeling swallowed my whole body—this was much worse than a ruined baseball card. All the people were gone. Had they escaped to a safer area? Did they all get eaten by a horrible monster? Maybe I would never find out the truth.

A faint thumping sounded in the distance, which sent ripples speeding across the footprint-shaped lakes. Then suddenly the noise got louder—sonic booms that felt like an earthquake had just hit. Sean toppled over and rolled down the hill. A beast was coming!

"What's going on?" Sean asked, hopping up and brushing himself off. "Why doesn't everything look all futuristic?"

"Something's wrong!" I answered. "We've changed the course of time, just like Mr. O warned. But how could saving all those people cause *this* to happen?"

A sudden thundering crash opened up a gaping hole in the ground beneath us, thick clouds of dust spewing out of it. Paul fell in, but he managed to grab the side, and he dangled over the bottomless pit. The

backpack slipped off his shoulder—TimeQuest 2 comic, Honus Wagner card and all—and disappeared into the dust. Paul's hands clutched the side of the cliff, his red, strained fingers quickly slipping toward the edge.

"Hold on!" I screamed as Sean and I grabbed Paul's hands. We dragged him out, ripping his shirt on the sharp edge, and quickly scrambled away from the hole just as another quake sent an avalanche of rocks tumbling into it. I looked down at Paul lying on the ground, gasping for breath. Suddenly, one baseball card didn't seem as important as my best friend, who never complained about all the dangers I put him in. I helped him to his feet and untied the backpack, which was tangled around his foot by the straps.

"Close call," Paul said, supporting himself on my shoulder. "Thanks."

A gargantuan foot landed nearby, which splashed up a huge mound of dirt. We immediately dove behind it. I peeked out and saw the monstrous appendage. It had seven green claws, each as long as a car. The toes were huge red bones connected to a shiny, cherry-like ball with protruding spikes. The whole thing was just one foot, yet it was bigger than my house—or what *had been* my house.

We sat in perfect silence behind the dirt pile, hoping whatever it was would just continue on its way. The mace-like limb was the creature's lone back foot, which it planted wherever it wanted to go. Then with

a grunting, gurgling, hissing, bleating, ground-shaking leap, it swung over the rest of its hideous body, which landed on two smaller front legs. Its massive head bobbed down, and two black tusks scraped against the pebbles. While staring blankly through glowing red eyes, it dug a creature out of the ground and tossed it into its mucus-filled mouth.

My heart pounded as the hulking beast's shadow left us in darkness. The nightmarish thing had a large spine that oozed black liquid onto its wrinkly yellow skin. As the goop sizzled and disappeared into pores, a horrible smell enveloped us and we held our noses. When the monster let out an ear-splitting cry, I closed my eyes and wished we were back on the warm, safe *Titanic*.

The horrible stench made Paul want to sneeze. He held his nose, but it came out anyway (partly through his ears, I think). The monster's bony neck extended a ridiculous distance, curving around our dirt mound until its snarling face nearly touched us. It let out a cry a zillion times louder than Dad's after I destroyed his baseball card, and a ring of sharp horns emerged from its head, creating a deadly crown.

"Run!" I said as its back foot swung over and crushed our safety mound. The three of us ran as fast as we could, desperately weaving between the lakes, with no idea of where we were headed, and pebble wreckage crunching under our feet the whole way. Moments later the beast's back foot slammed down behind us, creating a shower of dirt that knocked me to the ground. Sean and Paul pulled me up just before the monster's tusks slammed down. We ran around aimlessly, but soon we were out of breath and no closer to safety. It all seemed hopeless. Was this the same fate that all the people in the crushed houses had met?

"Over this hill," I said. With the thing right behind us, shrieking, drooling, and dripping slimy mucus, we put our last hope in a small rocky ridge ahead. When the monstrosity launched one of its sharp horns at us like a spear, we dove over the hill and rolled down an embankment, where we made another horrible discovery—a vast crater full of creatures identical to the one chasing us. Each one dug away at the earth with its tusks, extracting rocks, roots, and trees, crushing them into a black liquid, and then rolling around in the brackish mud.

We dove into a nearby cave just as all the creatures in the crater looked up and hissed at the newcomer, apparently angry that another monster was trying to barge in on their territory. Our pursuer suddenly disappeared, leaving us in the safety of the dark cave.

"What are we going to do?" I asked as we scrambled deeper into the cave. Paul pulled a lighter out of his backpack and made a small torch out of a hunk of wood. He stuck it in the ground, and we flopped down around the fire, too tired to clean the dirt and mucus from our clothes.

"We've wrecked the world," Paul said. "I knew we shouldn't have messed with time. Let's check the TimeQuest 2 comic. Maybe it'll explain how this happened." He pulled it out of his backpack and flipped to the last page we had read.

More pages of the cartoon panels had filled in, showing when Dr. Grim chased us around the boat for a blood sample and when we tricked Captain Smith into watching the movie. Large beads of sweat flew off Paul's body as he steered the *Titanic* around the iceberg, a determined look on his face. A colorful two-page spread showed our dramatic encounter with the monster after we warped back to the present. One caption read "Will the giant miasmas eat our three heroes, or will they escape from the cave and somehow return the space-time continuum to normal? Read on to find out!"

"Are those monsters miasmas?" Paul asked. We looked at Sean.

"I didn't do anything!" Sean said, shrugging his shoulders. He flipped the page in the comic. "Look, fellas, more of the story appeared!" He pointed to the next page, which had entirely filled in with text: "As our unsuspecting heroes try to place the blame for what has happened to the course of history, the truth eludes them. Will they realize that they alone are responsible for monsters taking over the world? Do they even have the slightest clue that by saving the *Titanic* they doomed the rest of mankind? You, reader, may be wondering how such a thing could happen. It's quite simple, really." A small diagram appeared, showing a sequence of events.

By saving the Titanic, our heroes also saved the life of the **VAMPIRE** *Dr. Alice Grim, who otherwise would have been eternally frozen inside a block of ice when the ship sank. After tasting dragon's blood acquired on the Titanic, she became intrigued with the flavor. At her summer castle in New York, she performed a series of experiments in her laboratory. Little did she know that the dragon's blood, festering in the hot, steamy hold of the ship, contained tiny*

microbes that, when mixed with chemicals, spawned a terrible monstrosity. At first the beast was no bigger than a test tube, but before long it grew and grew and grew, until it burst out of the lab and unleashed its terror upon the world.

The creature, known as a miasma, multiplied rapidly and became the dominant life form on Earth over the next century. The beasts feed on all carbon-based organisms and have a great need to lubricate their exoskeletons with brackish oils extracted from fossils and rocks. Can our heroes possibly have guessed that this is what their actions have led to? Will they find a solution? Read on to find out!

Paul and I glared at Sean.

"I didn't do anything!"

We Journey to Earth 2

Safe inside the cave, hidden away from the grotesque eyes of the feeding miasmas, we desperately read the TimeQuest 2 comic in hopes of finding another clue. I turned the page, only to see two holographic advertisements jump out at me in 3-D. The first showed a big green sphere with a blue eye painted on it. Colorful waves crashed against the sphere from all sides. A deep voice said, "Lord Anddo is watching you! Isn't there something you've forgotten to do? Watch your step. The black wave is hungry!"

"What's that an ad for?" I asked as I put my hand into the hologram to see if I could touch it. Everybody shrugged and my arm went right through it.

I peered into the second ad. It showed a boy and a girl sitting in front of a small silver cube, which said in a high-pitched voice, "The number of planets in the universe with intelligent life is 2,714. Ask me another question." The two excited kids turned to me and winked. The girl patted the cube and pressed a purple button on it.

The boy suddenly said, "Have you ever wanted to know the answer to a question, but you couldn't find it on the neural-thought network? Introducing the Answer Box, a device that can answer any question about the past or present! Our patented technology can tap into the infowave, a previously unknown energy field hidden within the dark matter of the universe. This dynamic field records everything that has ever happened in the universe, and is accessible from anywhere. Did you know that there are 171,124 buried treasure chests waiting to be found on all planets? And that besides boys and girls, there are also brilgoys? Could you ever have guessed that 191 people in the universe are named Graklfragl? (189 girls, 1 boy, and 1 brilgoy). Or that there are 800,000,910,127,111 bees in the universe? These are only a few of the questions that have been answered using the amazing Answer Box! Buy yours today for only 100 purple coins."

The girl then added in a fast-talking voice, "Answer Box Incorporated is not responsible or liable for horrible things that can result from learning secrets about your friends, family, or the universe. Use the Answer Box wisely—do not ask it any questions you do not really want to know the answer to, such as 'What is the most disgusting thing I ever ate without knowing it?' A complete list of safety instructions can be obtained by writing to: Answer Box, a division of TimeQuest 2 Inc., TimeQuest Beach, Earth 2, 100,000 A.D."

"In the old days, comics had ads for a big box of plastic soldiers for a dollar," Paul said.

"That's it!" Sean said, snapping his fingers. "All we have to do is warp to the year 100,000, buy one of those Answer Boxes, and ask it how we can fix the world!"

"He's right," Paul said. "Only a supercomputer can save us. We'll never figure it out on our own."

"Indeed," Sean said, raising his head proudly. "Good thing I came along. You fellas need my tricky smarts."

Just then, part of the cave mouth collapsed, and a giant miasma's face appeared, with black oil dripping from a dented tusk. One of its front limbs began groping for us, creating avalanches of boulders.

"Let's go now!" I ordered as we dove out of the way of falling rocks. "Bracelet! Take us to Earth 2 in the year 100,000!"

The miasma's claw ripped a large gash across that nightmarish world, creating a hole in the space-time continuum that quickly sucked us in like an interdimensional vacuum cleaner. It immediately spit us out onto a crowded sandy beach next to a multicolored ocean. Green, red, and orange waves lapped gently against the shore. Some kids rode them with electronic surfboards, while others built big castles in the sand. Adults lay around on computerized towels, gazing up at the starry black sky. The green, glowing sphere with the giant eye

that we had seen in the TimeQuest ad sat on the horizon, with giant purple and pink waves crashing against it. There was no sun, but the whole place glowed green because of light beaming from the sphere.

"22.1 miles per hour, with a wave height of 3.2 feet, and one 360-degree turn accomplished," a surfboard told a blond-haired girl who walked out of the water carrying it under her arm. "Would you like to see the instant replay?"

"No thanks, Cybrax, I'm done surfing for now," she said, walking over to us.

"As you wish, Shannz. Always a pleasure."

"Where are we?" Paul asked the girl.

"Why, Earth 2, of course," she replied, dropping the surfboard on the sand.

"Ow," the surfboard complained. "You always do that."

"Welcome to our planetoid," Shannz continued. "You're not from here, are you?" she said, eyeing our clothes. I looked around and realized that everybody on the beach was wearing a shiny silver bathing suit.

"Is there a city nearby where we can buy something?" I asked. "We need to get an Answer Box to help us with a quest we're on." I scampered over a nearby dune to see if I could get a better view of the planet.

"I wouldn't walk that way," Shannz said calmly.

After a few short steps, the dune suddenly ended, and I fell right off the edge of the world! I grabbed a long weed and swung helplessly back and forth at the planet's edge. My palms got sweaty immediately. Paul and Sean ran over and tried to pull me up. That's when I noticed that this world was completely flat. The mysterious green sphere poked out of the bottom of Earth 2, and hundreds of tubes with large suction cups connected the sphere to the underside of the planet.

"Hang on!" Paul yelled. He tried to yank the weed I was holding, but the world's sharp edge cut it, and I plummeted down into empty space! As I fell, the air became thin and I started choking. My heart pounded as I saw the strange planetoid above me grow

more distant. Lightheaded and dizzy, I wondered if Christopher Columbus would be surprised that Earth 2 was flat.

"Foolish boy," Shannz said faintly from above. A giant net zoomed down, caught me in its webbing, and pulled me back up to the surface of the planetoid. I fell at Shannz's feet. Seconds later she pressed a button on her bathing suit, causing the net to release me and then disappear into the silvery fabric around her waist. Relieved, I took a desperate gulp of air.

"How could this world be flat?" I gasped, trying to convince my shaky legs to let me stand up.

"Round, flat, cube, they're just geometric shapes," Shannz said.

"But what about gravity and orbits around the sun and all that stuff?" Paul asked.

"The energy sphere gives us all we need to live," she replied, gesturing toward the glowing ball at the horizon. Its giant eye seemed to be frowning at me. "It makes gravity under us with giant suction cups, and it evaporates water into oxygen so we can breathe."

"Enough small talk," Sean said. "Do you know where we can get an Answer Box? We have a world to save."

"How utterly predictable," Shannz said. "Boys trying to save Earth 1 from certain doom. Those TimeQuest bracelets you're wearing are the real problem. Time-traveling kids like you caused Earth 1's orbital shift in the year 77,340. More recently, kids tried to go back in time to prevent Earth 1 from splitting in half after the great centimillennial fireworks of 99,999. Only now the planet is in twelve pieces, one of which plummeted into the Sun! The survivors of Earth 1 are scattered all over the universe. Lord Anddo created this planetoid as a way of keeping Earth's traditions alive—over one billion former Earthlings now populate its beaches."

"You mean this place is just one big beach?" Paul asked. "Where are all the homes?"

"We live at the beach. The sand is edible, and the water is drinkable. It's always the perfect temperature out. The only things we have to watch out for are Lord Anddo's monsters. But we're prepared for them." She pressed a button on her shiny bathing suit, and a whole bunch of laser beams shot out of sparkling gemstones embedded in the fabric and disappeared into outer space. Moments later she pressed the button again and the laser beams stopped. I looked around at the kids frolicking in the surf, eating the sand, and drinking the water. Fun at the beach for an eternity. Weird.

"You don't go to school?" I asked. Sean kneeled down and tasted a glob of sand. He pulled a saltshaker out of his pocket, sprinkled salt on the sand, and then ate some more.

"Our minds are connected to the neural-thought network," Shannz continued. "We each have the collected knowledge of humankind in our heads at all times. Lord Anddo disapproves of the network and sometimes sends cybersaurs into it to shut it down. I sure have headaches on those days."

"Can you tell us where we can get an Answer Box already! Or at least some futuristic ice cream?" Sean whined. "All you do is talk, talk, talk!"

Shannz stared at Sean intently but didn't say anything. She looked at him for a long time, until Sean blinked rapidly and rubbed his eyes.

"I just *thought* the answer to you, Earth 1 boy," Shannz began, "but I guess you're not connected to the neural-thought network."

"OK, fine, you can talk!" Sean yelled. "But make it short. Miasmas are eating Earth 1."

"Typical," she said, shaking her head. "Lord Anddo banned Answer Boxes because they threatened his power. Only one Answer Box remains inside the energy sphere. Lord Anddo rules over us with an iron fist and punishes those who don't obey the laws of our world. He has recently seized TimeQuest 2 Inc. and takes special pleasure in collecting the many debts that children owe that company."

Paul and I looked at each other with wide eyes. Before either of us could say anything, a miniature pyramid lifted out of the sand and hovered next to us, speaking in a droning voice:

"Debtors detected on Sister Beach. Brian and Paul owe one octillion, two hundred seventy-one septillion, two hundred forty-six sextillion, two hundred ninety-six

quintillion, four hundred seventy-two quadrillion, five hundred sixty-three trillion, four hundred thirty-two billion, one hundred twelve million, one hundred thirty-four thousand, nine hundred ninety-nine purple coins to TimeQuest 2 Inc. regarding a loan initiated on Earth 1 in the year 2002 in the amount of one purple coin. Since you have failed to make any effort at all to repay this loan, you will now be brought to Lord Anddo to face your punishment!" The pyramid sank back into the sand.

"It must be from that one coin we owed because your underwear wasn't worth enough!" Paul said frantically. "The interest really does add up over thousands of years!"

My face felt warm as Shannz looked at me and giggled. How humiliating! Now she knew that Mom bought my underwear at a dollar store!

Suddenly, a black mound rose up at the horizon, right next to the glowing green sphere, and quickly turned into the largest wave I had ever seen. It devoured a low-flying comet as it raced toward us. Bloodshot eyes appeared in the middle of the wave. Men, women, and children screamed and jumped onto their surfboards, clearing the beach in a few minutes. Even the littlest kids skillfully rode multicolored waves, from one to another, until they were out of sight.

"Oh, great, now you've involved me in your mischief!" Shannz announced. "Cybrax, get ready."

"Not the black wave," the surfboard moaned.

"I'm afraid so, Cybrax." Shannz pressed a few buttons on the board, making it grow longer. A cold darkness fell over us as the wave blocked out the warm glow of the energy sphere. "Everybody hop onto my surfboard, now!"

We Surf the Black Wave

As soon as we hopped onto Shannz's computerized surfboard, the angry wave curled into a towering breaker. Shannz steered Cybrax onto the black water and surfed down the dark tunnel that formed around us. Clutching each other, we zipped toward a green circle of light in the distance while the wave disintegrated behind us, crashing onto the beach with thunderous roars. When Shannz pressed a button with her foot, the board reached warp speed, shooting out the exit. My mouth was stuck open in a permanent scream as we did a few loops in the air and landed on top of the black wave.

"Huh?" the wave grunted, looking up at us with enormous eyes.

"That's right, Blacky, it's me," Shannz said. "You weren't planning on kidnapping these boys, were you?"

"Orders are orders, Shannz," the black wave replied. "Now why don't you run along and let them face their punishment. Lord Anddo does not need to see you."

"That's not surprising to hear," Shannz said. "But I can't abandon these boys, no matter how foolish they might be." She pressed a button on her bathing suit and launched a blue ray into the wave. A glassy barrier quickly rose up and deflected the beam into outer space.

"I'm impressed that you would risk so much to defend three extraterrestrial boys," the wave said. "Oh, very well, Shannz, I'll let you tag along. But don't say I didn't warn you. Hang on!" The black wave suddenly grew taller, rising up so high we were lifted into outer space. All of Earth 2 was visible below us—one big ocean fringed by thousands of oddly shaped beaches, with the glowing sphere in the middle. As we continued to rise up, I read the giant handwritten signs that labeled each beach: Tickle Beach, Bouncy Beach, The Underground Grotto, Treasure Beach, Breakfast Beach, Lunch Beach, Fiery Dunes, Refuse Beach, Low-Gravity Beach, Whirlpool Beach, My Parents' Private Beach, and hundreds of others. Finally, the wave stopped growing, leaving us stranded atop the tallest water ride in the universe. A liquid slide curved all the way down to the planetoid's surface. We held on to each other tightly, balancing on Cybrax and trying not to tilt over the edge.

"Whatever you do, don't let go!" Shannz cried as we teetered over the lip of the watery precipice. I imagined the TV news brief: *Boy eats baseball card. Wave eats boy. Story at eleven.*

"Have a nice ride!" the wave said gleefully as a watery foot formed and kicked us over the edge. We tilted onto the super-slide. Seconds later, free fall! Accompanied by lots of screams, fingernails digging into each other's backs, my stomach jumping from my body and parachuting to safety, Paul sneezing once, my goose bumps joining together to form a goose mound, my hair uncurling and turning white (according to Sean), and I may have eaten a bug. When we reached the planetoid, Cybrax reported a speed of 233.2 miles per hour!

The spray hit me like sharp knives as the slide curved us upright, and we zipped along a looping water track that meandered all the way to the green energy sphere. Colorful fish jumped over us, a cyber-mermaid attempted to slap me with her metallic tail, and a giant computerized shark tried to eat us. Finally, the black wave ended abruptly at a ramp that launched Cybrax directly at the side of the energy sphere.

"Everybody lean left!" Shannz ordered. The surfboard tilted, and we glanced off the side of the sphere and sped past it. But the black wave re-formed into a huge wall on the far side, which deflected us right back at the sphere. Moments later we crashed through a bright green plasma field and tumbled onto a glass floor. Covered in sticky green goop, I lay on the floor and looked at the green-tinted world around me, hoping I hadn't broken any major bones.

"I have never wiped out before while surfing,"

Shannz said, helping me up. "Cybrax, are you hurt?"

"If *hurt* means all of your delicate inside components falling apart, then yes," it said. "Initiating repair sequence."

Amazingly, this hollow "sun" wasn't dangerous at all—the hot, gooey plasma that coated our bodies quickly dripped away, and we found ourselves in a cavernous chamber with an enormous staircase spiraling into a green haze above. Big shadowy waves splashed onto the outside of the sphere, but they didn't make a crashing noise—only a faint sizzling as the plasma boiled the water into oxygen.

"Hey, this is where the last Answer Box is," I said excitedly. "We're inside the sun!" Mom would really yell at me for my packing job on this adventure—no long pants, no hat, no SPF-one-million sun block.

"I assure you we do not want to be in here," Shannz said. "It can only mean punishment at the hands of Lord Anddo."

Shannz pressed a button on Cybrax, shrinking it back to a normal-sized surfboard. Then we began the long climb up the circular staircase. It had no handrails, so we walked single file, carefully avoiding the steps that were splattered with slippery plasma.

"That Answer Box better be at the top," Sean said. "And that Lord Anddo chap better be out to lunch."

"I doubt rulers of planets go out to lunch," I said. "He probably has stuff delivered."

We climbed for a long time until the staircase finally ended at a big, domed control room at the top of the sphere. A computerized panel blinked and beeped and whirred around us. Hundreds of tiny security monitors displayed scenes from around Earth 2—mostly of people playing at the beach or lounging on towels. Labels read "Neural-thought network infiltration module," "Black wave control module," "Mega-shark instruction chip," "Gravity flux," among thousands of others. An empty floating chair soared around the room, banging into walls. Sparks flew from the delicate equipment.

That's when I spotted it—a green pedestal next to a sign that read "The Last Answer Box." On top of the pedestal sat a small silver cube with a purple button.

"The Answer Box!" I shrieked, running over to it. I pressed the button on the cube, causing a series of computerized beeps. A high-pitched voice said, "Ask me a question!" A sudden chill overcame me. We had all the knowledge in the universe at our fingertips.

"Even the neural-thought network is old-fashioned compared to that little cube," Shannz said. "It's a shame Lord Anddo destroyed all the rest of them when he seized the company. It used to be my favorite toy."

"Let's try it out," Paul said eagerly. "Answer Box, what's my name?"

"Scanning info-wave," the Answer Box replied. Moments later the cube said, "Your full name is Paul Bartholomew Smith III."

"Your middle name's Bartholomew?" I asked. "You never told me that!"

"It never came up," Paul said, blushing.

"Answer Box," I began, "where's the nearest buried treasure to my house?"

"Oh, dear, your house on Earth 1 was destroyed by miasmas in the twentieth century," the Answer Box replied in a surprised tone.

"I mean, where my house used to be, before we changed things."

"Very well. In 1698 Captain Kidd buried twelve bronze chests ten paces north of Pirate's Rock, three feet under the ground. In 2002, this location would translate to fifty yards due south of the entrance to Kmart, under the parking lot."

"Can somebody remember that for when we get things back to normal? I don't have a pencil," I said. Suddenly, that imaginary news brief sounded like *Brian finds treasure and doesn't eat it. Story at eleven.*

"Let me try," Sean said, pushing me out of the way. "Are there any magic phrases that actually work? Y'know, like 'Open, Sesame' from the *Arabian Nights* tales?"

"Good question," the Answer Box replied. "Only one functioning magical phrase in the universe is recorded on the info-wave. It is 'SPANKY-SPANKY-SPANKY-FLEEBER-FOO!' Surprisingly, only three children in the history of the universe have ever recited it. When spoken, the phrase will bring you good luck for one day. Or, very rarely, it will create a tuna fish sandwich."

"Stop wasting time and ask it the question you came to ask it," Shannz scolded. "Answer Box, how can these foolish boys reverse the changes they made to the course of Earth 1's history and return things to the way they were before?"

"Scanning info-wave," Answer Box said. "That's a toughie. Using probability generator to predict infinite timelines. One moment, please." Strange holographic symbols flew out of the silver cube and twirled around in impossibly complex patterns. I held my breath and

hoped, for the sake of Earth, my friends, my parents, and all of humankind, that it would come up with an answer for how we could undo the horrible thing that we did to the planet.

Our Encounter with Lord Anddo

After a long, awkward silence, the Answer Box responded to our question:

"In order to reverse the TimeQuest 2 changes, you need to go back in time. However, you will recall that you may not return to 1912. One sequence of events will prevent the disaster. You must travel to April 22, 1861, when Dr. Alice Grim was eight years old. That day, accompanying her father, a traveling salesman, on a trip to Transylvania, Alice was bitten by a vampire and transformed into a vampire herself. Many years later, she began traveling the world as a doctor and pretended to cure rare diseases. She used her profession as a way to acquire human blood to quench her thirst. If you adventurers prevent her from getting bitten by the vampire in the first place, she will never grow up to become a doctor, never board the *Titanic*, and never accidentally create the hideous miasmas that took over the world. Now please don't ask me any more questions for a while."

"I can't go back to 1912?" Sean asked. "How will I ever go home? Why didn't you fellas tell me that?"

"We didn't want to upset you," I said, hanging my head in shame. "These TimeQuest bracelets have strict rules."

"We'll find a way," Paul said, trying to comfort him. "Maybe the TimeQuest 2 comic will give us a hint how to do it, or the Answer Box will tell us."

A giant winged *Tyrannosaurus rex* splootched through the roof of the plasma sphere, swooped down, and landed on the platform. As the huge hole in the energy field slowly oozed shut, the transparent wings of the beast retracted into its metallic body. A blond-haired boy with an upturned nose hopped off and plugged the

computerized beast into an outlet. He wore an oversized shirt with a picture of him on it and a caption that read "I rule the world but all I got was this lousy T-shirt!"

"Lord Anddo!" Shannz shouted. She got down on her hands and knees and looked at the floor.

"Intruders into my lair," Lord Anddo said, turning to look at us. "Answer Box, why didn't you warn me there were invaders here?"

"You didn't ask," the Answer Box said.

"I need an assistant," Lord Anddo said, sighing. The erratic floating chair swooped down and crashed into the boy, knocking him down. He got up, pressed a button on the chair, and brushed himself off. "I always forget to shut this thing off before I go to lunch."

"So you *do* go out to lunch!" Sean said. "I was right!"

"Silence! You will not speak until spoken to!" Lord Anddo shouted. He held two fingers out to Sean and closed his eyes. After a long silence, Lord Anddo peeked at Sean and appeared disappointed. Sean scratched his head in confusion.

"Did you feel any pain at all?" Lord Anddo asked.

"My leg itched a bit," Sean answered.

"I can't do it on a full stomach," Lord Anddo said. "Aren't you the kids that owe me more than an octillion purple coins from a loan of one purple coin in the year 2002?" He looked at me and Paul and tapped his foot.

"Um, can we get another day on that loan?" Paul asked.

"Aren't you rich enough?" Shannz asked, jumping to her feet. "These boys have a problem that could affect our whole world! Please listen to—"

"Silence!" Lord Anddo interrupted, holding out his hand. "Who invited you anyway, Shannz?"

"You can't shut me out of your life forever, Anddo," Shannz said. "I won't let you."

"Ooh, what are you going to do about it, zap me with your puny bathing suit ray? Now quiet. I shall make an example of these debtors." He cleared his throat and put his arms akimbo. "Why, just this morning a boy showed up who owed me a duodecillion purple coins from a TimeQuest loan that he took out during the Middle Ages. He begged for mercy. Using my diabolical mind powers, I turned him into a giant purple coin and rolled him right off the edge of the world! But I have something much more sinister planned for these boys, much more sinister indeed.

"But first, an observation," he continued, holding out his index finger. "People sit around on the beaches that I constructed, eating, sleeping, frolicking in the sea. And do they thank me for it? No! They think bad things about me on that vile neural-thought network so that I have to send C-Rex into the network to scare them. This is not what ruling the world should be like. Where's the honor? The respect? And why hasn't anybody kissed my feet yet?"

"Your feet are a little stinky," Answer Box replied.

"Who asked you?"

"Will you just listen to what these boys have to say?" Shannz shouted.

"C-Rex," Lord Anddo said, turning to the metal dinosaur, "you're my only friend." He leaned on the metallic green scales of the robotic monster. The dinosaur roared softly and licked his blond hair with its rusty tongue. Suddenly, C-Rex disappeared. Thousands of computerized red letters spelling "TimeQuest Change" scrolled through the air quickly and formed the exact shape of the beast. C-Rex flickered back and forth between the letters and its normal form, until it disappeared entirely in one big flash. Lord Anddo crashed to the floor.

"Oh no," Paul said. "The space-time continuum changes have caught up to us!"

"What happened?" Lord Anddo asked, scrambling to his feet.

"These boys have been waiting to tell you that they altered Earth 1's history using a TimeQuest 2 comic book," Answer Box began. "They changed it so that humans were eaten by monsters in the twentieth century on Earth 1. As a result, humans will go extinct, and you will never be born, will never create Earth 2, C-Rex, or any of your other inventions. That's why they are all disappearing." The floating chair suddenly disappeared with a flash while Lord Anddo looked around in shock.

"Those blasted TimeQuest comics!" he hollered. "I should have seized that threat to my empire sooner!"

Suddenly, the entire energy sphere flickered red, changing momentarily into hundreds of rows of the words "TimeQuest Change." I glanced at my TimeQuest bracelet, which scrolled the words "TimeQuest Error. Implementing backup algorithm. New warp time destination recommended."

"We have to warp, fast!" I cried as a burst of fear raced through me. Paul reached into his backpack and grabbed the last two TimeQuest bracelets. The energy sphere suddenly disappeared and we tumbled through the air in a terrifying free fall until we splashed into the ocean.

"I won't forget about that debt!" Lord Anddo shouted as the black wave lifted us up and created a calm watery platform. "Well, Answer Box, what do we do now?"

"I told these journeyers earlier," Answer Box said, floating next to me, sparking, sputtering, and making strange noises. "You must go back to April 22, 1861, to Transylvania and prevent the young Alice Grim from getting bitten by a vampire. You must create a new course of events for Earth's history to follow!"

I plucked the Answer Box out of the water and stuffed it in Paul's backpack. Paul handed out the TimeQuest bracelets to Shannz and Lord Anddo. As the ocean began flashing red, I said, "Bracelet, transport us to April 22, 1861, Transylvania!" At once everything became black, and we found ourselves falling through the air. ...

A Mysterious Coach Ride

We crash-landed on a moss-covered patch of ground in a dark forest. The full moon lit up silhouettes of distant mountain ranges, where wolves howled constantly, as if they already knew we were intruders in their territory. Gusts of wind made the tree limbs creak and rustle, and their long clawed branches swiped at us from every direction. Far above the treetops, an eerie castle sat on a shadowy crag. There was no doubt about it; we were in that creepy country from vampire lore—Transylvania.

A faint blue light illuminated a dirt road nearby. Next to the road, a poster was tacked to a tree, showing a crudely drawn sketch of a girl. It was written in many different languages, and the English one read: "Missing: Alice Grim, Age 8. Feared taken by the demons of the night. Please contact concerned parents at Bistritz Hotel with information."

"This is her," I said, scrambling to my feet and grabbing the poster. "Is everybody here?" I quickly took

126

attendance, reassured that we were on the right track: Me, Paul, Sean, Shannz, Lord Anddo, Cybrax.

"Yes," the Answer Box said from within Paul's backpack. "Except I was damaged by the seawater and am now functioning at a level of intelligence equivalent to that of fortune cookie inserts."

"I feel your pain," Cybrax said. "I have the functioning level of a plank of wood."

"Confucius said that it is better to be wounded in the flesh than in the mind," Answer Box replied. "Lucky numbers: 1, 2, 4, 8, 15, 37."

"OK, can we end the high-tech-toy support group and figure out where we are?" Paul asked, rubbing his stomach. "I'm hungry."

"So are they!" Sean added, pointing to a pack of fuzzy animals walking quietly out of the forest. Wolves! Unlike their distant brothers, these didn't howl. They just stared at us, unblinking, out of round white eyes. Dozens more followed, bathed in that mysterious blue glow, and soon we were surrounded. Why didn't we ever encounter chipmunks or bunnies on our adventures? We must be using the wrong time-travel company.

"I'll take care of this," Lord Anddo said, pointing two fingers at a wolf and closing his eyes, deep in concentration. The wolf tilted its head and looked at him. Without warning, three of the wolves growled and pounced on Lord Anddo, knocking him to the ground.

"Go away!" Shannz cried, hitting them with her

surfboard. The rest of the wolves snarled, revealing sharp fangs. We were all about to become dinner!

"SPANKY-SPANKY-SPANKY-FLEEBER-FOO!" I said. Lord Anddo looked up at me desperately. A tuna fish sandwich appeared, floating in the air. All the wolves pounced on it, snapping at each other in a feeding frenzy. Answer Box's lucky phrase worked!

"Run!" I shouted, pulling Lord Anddo to his feet. We ran onto the dirt road and sprinted down the dark path. Seconds later the wolves were chasing after us, hungry for more food.

"What were the chances of getting the tuna fish sandwich?" I said as we ran up a steep incline.

"What were the chances my powers wouldn't work *again*?" Lord Anddo said. "I must be too far from home."

One wolf suddenly started nipping at Paul's backpack, ripping a hole in the pouch that held the Honus Wagner card. It started chewing on the plastic case, trying to pull it out of the bag. I grabbed a rock and threw it at the beast. The rogue wolf backed off and was soon lost in the rest of the pack.

With a wave of wolves about to wash over us, we had only seconds before we were devoured. Then a lantern light appeared up ahead, bouncing around like a firefly. The sounds of horse hoofs and wagon wheels soon drowned out the growling.

"A wagon is coming!" Paul yelled. Two large horses appeared pulling a wooden coach. A driver with a long brown beard uttered an unusual, high-pitched sound, causing the wolves to scamper into the forest and disappear.

"I'll handle this!" Sean announced. While the rest of us scattered off the road, he put out his hand to stop the coach, a determined look on his face.

"Whoa, Nellie. Whoa, Smelly," the driver said, pulling the reins. The horses stopped right in front of Sean and licked his forehead. The driver took the lantern out of an iron ring and climbed down.

"Impressive diabolical superpowers," Lord Anddo said.

"It's how I stop the ice-cream cart back home," Sean said, blowing on his fingers and pretending to cool them down.

"Who goes there?" the driver said, stopping a short distance from us.

"Let me explain," I said, determined to tell the truth. "We're from the future and we're here to stop this little girl from getting bitten by a vampire." I showed him the poster. He walked up to us and held the lantern to our faces, looking carefully at each of us. He wasn't a man at all but a boy not older than fourteen! He wore a long straw beard. In the moonlight he seemed very pale and thin. A long tail of dark brown hair trailed in the back of his head and down his neck.

"You should not be wandering around on St. George's Eve. The witches, werewolves, and dragons are afoot," he warned. "I will take you to my master's home. You will not survive out here." He opened a creaky door and gestured for us to sit down in the damp, uncomfortable back seat. The enormous moon now completely surrounded the castle far above us, revealing the dark silhouette of its ancient stone towers.

"Is that Dracula's castle?" I asked as we climbed into the coach.

Without another word he slammed the door, hopped back into the driver's seat, and started the coach on its way again. Before long, the horses stopped at the place where we had first landed, near that glowing blue light. The driver jumped off the coach and ran into the forest carrying a shovel.

"What's he doing now?" Paul asked.

"Maybe he has to go to the bathroom," Sean replied.

The mysterious boy came back a few minutes later with a small, shiny gold box. He placed it between our feet in the coach. "On St. George's Eve, all treasures that were buried by past inhabitants of the forest are magically revealed." The boy had extremely pointy ears, and his eyes seemed to glow red.

"Is everybody in this country rich, then?" I asked, wondering whether this holiday could only be celebrated in Transylvania.

"The peasants fear the creatures of the dark," the boy replied. "They do not venture out on such a night as this." He slammed the door. When the coach started moving again, I carefully tilted up the lid of the gold box, revealing a pile of gleaming coins and large rubies that glittered in the moonlight. Suddenly, all the wolves in the forest howled at once. I slammed it shut.

We sat in silence for a long time as the coach wound its way up a mountain. Soon, we left the trees behind and were surrounded only by ghostly boulders. The horses clomped up an impossibly steep driveway flanked by cliffs on both sides. The castle loomed over us like a guardian of the bluff—it was half-ruined and sitting at the very edge of the mountain, its walls blending with the cliff face. One tall tower stretched to the moon, and high arching windows peered out everywhere. Strange—I thought I saw a ghost peek out from one of the windows. After I blinked a few times and rubbed my eyes, the vision disappeared.

"How can anyone live in such a ruined place," Lord Anddo said.

"Those who dwell at the castle within their hearts will never wake up to find it in ruins," the Answer Box replied. "Lucky numbers: 1, 2, 4, 8, 15, 37."

"Thanks a lot, Answer Box," Paul said, staring in awe at the creepy castle.

I looked down at my TimeQuest bracelet, which beeped and flashed all sorts of symbols. The frightening words "Future eradicated; protagonist protection program implemented" scrolled across the screen. Our bodies flashed red, green, purple, blue, and yellow momentarily as our forms were replaced with hundreds of rows of tiny glowing words: "Fatal TimeQuest Error—Emergency Response Needed." We looked at ourselves in confusion. I reached down to touch the shimmering digital text that formed my leg, and my arm went right through it!

Our driver looked back at us just as our bodies flashed back into their usual form. Shannz pressed a button on her bathing suit, transforming her outfit into a shiny gold shirt and long pants. As the wolves howled and the werewolves bayed and the dragons roared in the distance, I wondered what was scarier—heading to Dracula's castle or knowing we had only a short time left to save ourselves and the world.

We Meet the Count

The coach pulled through a massive archway into a shadowy area, where all the wings and towers of the castle joined together to form a stone courtyard. It was hard to believe that only a few people lived in this place—the vast fortress looked like it could be a hotel for vampires. I imagined the receptionist who would greet us: *"Would you like an underground crypt or just a coffin in your room? Garlic or nongarlic? Just follow that ghost over there. It'll show you to your room."*

The bearded boy helped us out of the coach and led us through a gargantuan wooden door, which he seemed to open easily, and then into a dim foyer. Tapestries depicting the ancient landscape of Transylvania and its past rulers hung on the walls, bathed in moonlight that shone through crumbling windows. Large staircases curled in different directions—most of them decaying and impassable. Dozens of doors waited to be pushed open on their rusty hinges. A blazing fire lit up one side of the room, tossing around jittery shadows.

"My master is attending to business right now, but I shall show you to the guest quarters while you await his return." He pulled a cobwebby candelabra off the wall and led us up the rightmost staircase, down a long corridor, and into a hall of rooms perched at the very edge of the cliff. A series of big windows overlooked the Carpathian Mountains and the vast wilderness of trees that covered them.

"You may choose any of these rooms, but heed my warning," the boy began. "*Do not* venture into other parts of the castle. Enjoy your stay!"

"What about dinner?" Paul asked, rubbing his stomach.

"Sup?" the boy asked.

"Not much, how's it going?" Paul replied.

"Sup?" the boy repeated.

"Fine, you?" Paul said. "But what about food?"

"My English is not as it should be, though I have spent many hours in the library," the boy said. "A supper will be prepared for you by the kitchen staff. Perhaps it will be to your liking."

"Tell me," Lord Anddo said. "What does your master pay you? A servant would make my job so much easier."

"What line of employ are you in?" the boy asked, holding the candelabra to Anddo's face.

"Supreme ruler of the world," Anddo replied.

"Then, as with my master, no payment would be necessary. I serve out of loyalty and duty."

"I must meet your master," Lord Anddo replied. "We seem to have a lot in common."

"You most certainly will, in good time." He grinned at us, revealing a row of pointy teeth, with two unusually large fangs in the front. I felt a sudden chill, and I could see a momentary puff of my breath.

After the boy left us alone, we divided up the rooms. Sean claimed the largest suite—three octagonal chambers with a walk-in closet bigger than my house, and a balcony perched a thousand feet over the precipice. The suite had four fireplaces, each roaring with a newly lit fire. Sean hopped onto the fluffy bed, causing a plume of dust to fly up and form a cloud.

"Wake me for supper," Sean instructed, "unless it's something unpleasant, like squash. Squash ought to be squashed out of existence."

"I eliminated squash when I created Earth 2," Lord Anddo said. "I also did away with Brussels sprouts."

"What about cauliflower?"

"Too powerful," Anddo said, hanging his head in shame.

Shannz grimaced at Lord Anddo and then went into her room to work on repairing Cybrax and the Answer Box. Lord Anddo entered an adjoining room, announcing that he needed some quiet time to recharge his diabolical powers. Paul and I claimed two rooms overlooking the central tower, which seemed to howl on its own when wind whipped around its weathered stone turrets. We sat on the dusty bed in my room next to a roaring fire and eagerly read the TimeQuest 2 comic again, hoping it would give us a clue about what to do next.

"Look, more pages have filled in!" Paul said, pointing. "The comic's almost used up!" One giant box showed the flat world of Earth 2, with me falling off the edge, while Shannz sent her bathing suit net down to rescue me. Then a full-page spread showed us riding the black wave all the way down to the energy sphere, while the word "Yeaghhhhh!" came out of my mouth in a cartoon bubble. Another page showed the wide-eyed looks on our faces as the energy sphere disappeared and we plummeted into the ocean.

"More boxes are filling in!" I blurted, pointing to the next page. The pictures appeared right before our eyes. One showed saliva drooling from the mouths of the wolves as they pounced on the tuna fish sandwich. A box read "Could Brian even have guessed that there was only a one-in-twelve-billion chance of getting the tuna fish sandwich after reciting the magic phrase? That's like winning the lottery twenty times!"

Finally, a dramatic two-page spread showed the castle in Transylvania, with light glowing in the windows of the guest wing. A caption read "Can our heroes, Sean, Brian, Paul, Shannz, and her brother Anddo, prevent Alice Grim from being bitten by a vampire before it's too late? Or will the universe as we know it cease to exist? Read on to find out!"

"I didn't know Lord Anddo and Shannz were brother and sister!" Paul said.

"How are we going to get to Alice, even if she is here?" I asked. "That boy said we weren't allowed to leave the guest wing."

"Just because we're not allowed to doesn't mean we're not *going* to," Paul assured me. "And no, it doesn't count as lying to go against the rules of some weird kid with a straw beard in Transylvania. Don't even try to say that it does."

"I guess," I said reluctantly. "But I wish we could just relax here for a few minutes and roast marshmallows in one of these fireplaces." I pulled the Honus

Wagner card out of Paul's backpack just to look at it for a minute. The plastic case had seawater, black miasma goop, green plasma, teeth marks, and slobber all over it, but the card was still in mint condition inside. Was destroying the whole course of humanity worth one tiny little million-dollar baseball card?

I suddenly envisioned the press conference at the end of our journey: *"You nearly destroyed the world for a piece of painted cardboard?"* a concerned reporter asked me as I stood in front of a bunch of microphones. *"Yet you still expect to receive this World's Best Son award."* Dad pushed the reporters away, shouting, *"Stay back, he bites!"*

Paul snapped his fingers in front of my face. "Earth 2 to Brian."

"Fine, let's go exploring," I said, jolted back to reality. "But first we'll tell the others."

We darted out the door and ran right into the count of the castle! I fell to the ground in surprise and stared up at him for a moment. He wore a large black cape that formed a collar near his unusually pointy ears. He had a long tail of brown hair that streamed down his back, and he was very pale. His eyes seemed to flicker red in the firelight. That's when I noticed a strange thing—he was only a boy, about the same age as the one that drove us to the castle!

"Good evening," he said, helping me to my feet. His hands were as cold as ice. "I trust Allak has made you comfortable. He tells me you were in trouble on the mountainside. The wolves would have devoured you before dawn—my pets are always hungry."

"Your pets?" Paul asked.

"I mean, my *pests*," the boy said, licking his bright red lips. "Er, *those* pests. Those pests are always hungry. Are *you* inclined to sup? The kitchen staff has prepared a roast chicken stuffed with squash."

"Are you the boy that drove us here?" Paul asked directly. "Because you look like him, only now you have a cape and no beard."

"Nonsense, that was my faithful servant Allak," he said, walking up to me so close that I could feel his icy breath. He leaned over and sniffed my neck. "You have a far-off scent," he said.

"Are you Dracula?" I asked.

"Vlad Dracula was a violent and cruel man who ruled these parts in the fifteenth century. I am named Mirkea the Great, after the man who died bravely trying to free our country. I knew both men well, and I insist that you call me Count Mirkea."

"You knew them, and they ruled in the fifteenth century?" I asked. "But you're almost our age." Count Mirkea's eyes glowed brighter, and he scratched his neck nervously. His fingernails were sharp, and he had hair on the palms of his hands! Perhaps it wasn't such a good idea to argue with this boy after all.

"Uh, I have read of their deeds in my library on many a lonely night," he said. "I have met them a

hundred times over in the pages of my books. Now gather your allies, for dinner, as you call it, is served." He walked down the hallway and disappeared quickly, his footsteps making no sound on the stone floor. The only noise came from a key ring full of rusty iron keys that clanked around his waist.

I walked into Shannz's room, hoping she had fixed the Answer Box. I had so many more questions to ask it: Was Count Mirkea the same boy that drove us to the castle? Was he really the young Dracula? *Were* there boy vampires in the world? Just then, Lord Anddo walked through the adjoining doorway, rubbing his eyes.

"I almost fixed Answer Box, everyone," Shannz said proudly. "It can answer questions again, but for some reason it can only speak in early twenty-first-century slang. Listen!" She pressed a button on the silver cube and it suddenly said in a gruff voice, "Ask me a question, yo!"

"Answer Box, is Count Mirkea that kid who drove us to the castle, or is he a vampire?"

"Yo G, that pale dude ain't straight-up, and he be whack, bro!" the Answer Box replied. We all looked at each other in confusion.

"Answer Box, does he really have Alice Grim locked up in this castle somewhere? Is he going to turn her into a vampire?" I asked.

"Sho'nuff, that pale dude 'bout to beast out on the homey cattywompus to the bling-bling," Answer Box said. I looked at Paul for a translation, but he just shrugged his shoulders.

"C'mon, let's go to dinner," Paul urged, rubbing his stomach. "The count is waiting. Somebody go wake Sean."

An Unusual Meal

We ate dinner in a large candlelit chamber overlooking the shadowy courtyard. A wooden table spanned the whole room, and a huge mirror hung on the wall opposite the windows, making the dining hall seem even bigger. Count Mirkea sat at one end of the table, wearing a black cloak with large fuzzy spiders crawling on it and weaving shiny webs. A burnt chicken sat on the table with green goop dripping off it.

"Enjoy your meal, for it might be your last," Count Mirkea said, tossing a piece of chicken out the window. I heard the growling, jaw-snapping whimper of hungry wolves. We all dropped our silverware and stared at him in shock. His eyes opened wide, and he shot to his feet, saying nervously, "Your last meal *in this castle*, I meant to say. After all, you're here only to escape the dangers of the night. And the sun shall soon rise."

I breathed a sigh of relief, but I suddenly remembered how tired I was. I hadn't slept since we were on the *Titanic*, except for a few minutes of dozing on the ride to the castle.

"How is your chicken stuffed with squash?" the count asked. "It's a little dish my chef learned on a trip to England."

"Squash! That evil weed!" Sean cried, tossing down his fork and spitting out a green blob. "I told you not to wake me if the supper had squash in it!"

"We forgot," Paul admitted.

Sean got up and walked toward the kitchen, mumbling something about the chef.

"I kinda like it," I said, nibbling on a charred drumstick. At that moment I noticed a yellowish bristly mass sticking out the back of the stuffed chicken, as if a porcupine had crawled into it. I leaned over to the serving tray and pulled on the thing carefully, until it popped out. It was a fake straw beard! Everybody dropped their silverware again, and Paul started gagging.

Count Mirkea's eyes opened wide and he stood up quickly.

"So you *were* the driver of that coach!" I said. "You've been lying to us!"

"If you must know, my servant Allak is incompetent, so I've been filling in for him. My apologies, but it isn't right for a count of a castle to be doing the work of a peasant. I shan't lie again."

Suddenly, Sean came running back into the room, as pale as a ghost. "There is no chef!" he cried. "The kitchen's all covered in cobwebs, and there's no more food in there."

"You cooked this meal?" I asked Count Mirkea.

"Yes, yes, I did!" he answered angrily. His voice took on a demonic fury, and his eyes glowed red. The air turned cold, and the hairs on my arm stood on end. "It's been many years since I've had the pleasure of company at supper. Is it a crime to be a lonely orphan, dwelling in this ancient, crumbling castle alone? Even the dust has dust in this accursed place. Thanks to the actions of my ancestors and the way I look, I've been branded as a vampire! Nobody will dare serve me! I tried to turn the castle into a tourist attraction just to have some people around. But only three people ever bought tickets. Two of them were eaten by wolves and the last one's still lost in the never-ending hedge maze. Did I save your lives, only to earn your distrust?"

"Fine, I'm sorry," I said, suddenly feeling bad for the count. "But no more lies." Maybe he really was just a lonely kid. And it's not his fault that he has nobody to take care of him. And he did save us from those wolves—if he wanted to hurt us or to suck our blood like vampires do, why hadn't he done it already? Was he a vampire after all, or was that part of his tourist attraction?

We ate quietly for a while, glancing awkwardly at each other. Straw beard aside, the meal wasn't really that bad. It had a tangy flavor. Sean whispered with

Lord Anddo for a long time, occasionally slapping his left palm with his right fist. I overheard the words "world domination" and "squash."

"Aren't you going to eat anything, Count Mirkea?" Shannz asked.

"I don't eat solid food," Count Mirkea said, licking his bright red lips. "I'm on a liquid diet. It's how I maintain my slender figure." He lifted up his cloak to show us his skinny chest, which had large rib bones protruding from it. "I also jog from the festering crypt to the belfry three times a day."

I glanced at the giant mirror on the wall. It reflected the entire table with everyone sitting at it, but the count was nowhere to be seen! He didn't show up at all in the reflection, even though his empty chair did!

"Your reflection doesn't show up in that mirror!" I shrieked, standing up and pointing to the count. Paul looked at me worriedly.

"Relax. That mirror hasn't reflected properly ever since I bought it at a garage sale." The count gathered a few strands of cobwebs from his cloak and used them to tie his mane of hair into a brown pigtail.

"*Are* you a vampire?" I asked. "Answer truthfully." Everybody stared at him expectantly. A rooster crowed somewhere in the distance, and through the windows I could see the dim orange glow of morning peeking over the mountaintops.

"Time for bed!" Count Mirkea chimed. He swung

his cape over his face and fled the room, his key ring jingling around his waist. We were left with a half-eaten green-and-black chicken, a growling sea of wolves at the window, and a lot of questions about our host.

"I don't get it. If he's a vampire, how come he hasn't drunk our blood already?" I asked.

"Another moment and I would've zapped him with my mega-thought blast," Lord Anddo said, holding out both hands and connecting his index fingers.

"Oh, would you stop pretending!" Shannz cried. "You *don't* have any powers!"

"You're just jealous that I'm supreme ruler of the world and you're not."

"What world?" Shannz said. "It's probably disappeared by now, and it's our responsibility to fix things. Did you even say good-bye to Mom on the neural-thought network before we left? You say you have these great powers, but all you do is terrorize people with the monsters that I helped you build!"

"So you really *are* brother and sister," Paul interjected.

"Try to convince him of that," Shannz retorted. "He won't even toss a thought packet to me unless he needs me to repair something."

"I'm talking to you now, even though I'd rather be getting bitten by a vampire," Lord Anddo sneered, crossing his arms.

"Zap me with a mega-thought blast if you can,"

Shannz said. "I dare you!" She held out her arms like wings and closed her eyes.

Lord Anddo pointed at Shannz with both hands, connecting his index fingers. We watched in silence as a pained look overcame Anddo's face, contorting his expression and turning his face bright red. A blood-curdling scream came from somewhere high up in the castle.

"I must have missed," Anddo said, looking at his fingers.

"Alice Grim!" I shrieked. "She's here after all. She must be locked up in the tower!"

"We'll have to duel again some other time, Sis," Lord Anddo said, smiling at her.

Shannz sneered at him, and then we abandoned the dining room and ran into the castle foyer. A staircase made out of blue stones had a sign that read "Please Do Not Feed the Bats in the Belfry." We ran up the steep, curving stairwell. Unfortunately, it ended abruptly at a locked wooden door with another sign, "Closed for Repairs." A complicated combination lock with six separate antique dials was imbedded in the door.

"How are we going to get through this door?" Paul asked, kicking it.

"Answer Box, what were those lucky numbers you mentioned earlier?" Shannz asked as she pulled the shiny cube out of her pocket.

"A-yo, diggity dank, I dish out da digits," Answer Box replied. "Dey be 1, 2, 4, 8, 15, 37."

"Thanks, Answer Box," Shannz said, putting it back in her pocket.

"LOL, it's kewl, homey. Now I be chillaxin in dis pocket till you need the 411."

We carefully set the corroded dials to the numbers that Answer Box gave us. When I pulled the large metal handle, a loud clank came from inside the door, and it creaked open on rusty hinges. We ran up the gloomy tower, which had dusty stairs that wound up for what seemed like an eternity. Mice scrambled out of dark corners as we jumped the steps two at a time. Out of breath, we finally came to a circular landing at the top, which opened into four locked prison cells. I peeked through the bars of one of the doors and saw a big pile of gold and jewels inside. The count's treasure!

"That's what Answer Box was trying to tell us earlier," I said. "Alice Grim is opposite the treasure!" Next to the riches stood a sloppy, hand-painted sign that read "Please Do Not." I turned around and ran toward another closed prison door. A bunch of bats flew out of it and escaped through an arched window.

"Thank you for scaring off the bats," a little girl said from behind the bars. She had curly black hair and looked like a miniature version of Dr. Grim from the *Titanic*, minus the fangs, I hoped.

"Are you Alice Grim?" Sean asked.

"Yes, my mummy and poppa were traveling, selling garlic and spices to village traders, when a pack of

wolves overtook our coach and dragged me away. That awful Count Mirkea locked me up here and won't let me go." She clutched a wooden doll with short black hair and a painted face.

"Vampire bite check," Paul said immediately.

At once Shannz examined Alice's neck through the prison bars. "No bites," she concluded. "We made it in time!"

"Your parents are at the Bistritz Hotel," I reassured the girl. "They've been searching for you." I showed her the crumpled poster that I had taken from the tree in the forest.

"Please help me," Alice said. "The count wants to drink my blood—it's all he talks about. I have been able to hold him off only with this bag of garlic from my father's stock." She showed me a small canvas bag that was tied to her waist and smelled pungent.

"That's a vampire's weakness, one of them anyway," Paul explained. "Every hero or villain has one. Superman's weakness is kryptonite, the werewolf is afraid of silver bullets, vampires are repelled by garlic and daylight, and Popeye hates spinach."

"Popeye *likes* spinach because it makes him strong," I retorted.

"I never heard of Popeye," Sean said, "but spinach tastes like swamp slime!"

"Never mind that right now. Do you know where the key to this door is?" I asked, jiggling the rusty iron doorknob.

"Count Mirkea has it on a key ring that he carries with him everywhere," Alice said. "He always goes to sleep at dawn, so now would be a good time to steal it."

"OK. Shannz and Anddo, you stay here and guard Alice," I ordered. "The rest of us will go and see if we can get that key."

"Be careful, there are ghosts about," Alice said.

"Don't worry, we're here with you now," Shannz said, holding her hand. "Everything will be all right."

As I ran back down the stairs with Paul and Sean, I wondered if Alice Grim could ever understand that her destiny also determined the fate of Earth. If we could prevent her from being transformed into a vampire, then she will never carry out that awful experiment when she gets older—the one that spawned the mias-mas that destroyed the world. How do you explain to an eight-year-old girl that all that stood between us and saving the world was a small metal key!

When we reached the castle foyer, only one staircase remained that wasn't a heap of crumbled stones—a dark one that led down into the depths of the castle. A dusty sign read "Festering Crypt—Proceed with Caution."

After taking a few careful steps down the black stones, a horrible smell overcame me. "I knew Count Mirkea was evil," I whispered, holding my nose.

"He seemed pretty cool," Paul said.

"I just hope he's a good sleeper," Sean said as we crept down the slippery stairs into the darkness.

We Journey into the Crypt

As we ventured into the depths of the castle, the staircase became more perilous, with crumbling steps, moss-covered stones, and slippery puddles. Small candles inside arched recesses in the wall barely illuminated my feet. Deeper still, a green mist blanketed the ground and traveled toward the ceiling in wispy tendrils. An oozing, slurping sound came from all around us, and the air smelled like rotting vegetables.

"No wonder Count Mirkea didn't get many tourists," I remarked.

"He probably sleeps in the darkest, smelliest, coldest place in the castle," Paul said.

At that moment Sean stepped on something, hidden under the blanket of mist, that made a loud squishing noise. He struggled to pull his foot up—a black, gelatinous mass appeared briefly, then seconds later I heard a loud slurping sound and an echoing burp.

"Some blob just ate my shoe!" he said, kicking the

creature with his other foot. There was another brief slurp, and then a burp. "I'm shoeless!" He lifted his left foot and showed us his sock, which was mostly eaten away and covered in black slime.

"Walk faster!" I ordered as something bumped into my foot under the heavy mist. We darted down the rest of the staircase, while ancient steps collapsed under our feet and strange creatures woke up and scurried around.

We finally emerged in a misty graveyard on a lower plateau of the cliff. Statues of nightmarish creatures sat among weeds and gravestones—a giant bat with a dragon's head, a three-headed wolf with tusks, a white ghost that seemed to blink at us, and a medieval knight with a lizard's tail. Mixed in with these strange beasts were an ordinary stone cow and frog. Overgrown bushes and weeds grew between all the graves, covering them with strawberries, blueberries, raspberries, and dozens of other fruits. Even though we were outside, a permanent cloud covered the sun, casting us in a greenish gloom.

"Look!" Sean cried, pointing to a large stone crypt at the far end of the garden. A flaming torch lit up a circular, moss-covered building with a flight of stairs leading down into darkness.

"That's gotta lead to the count's bedroom," I said. "Just like in the movies." We walked quickly toward it. Working our way through the thickets, we casually plucked strawberries and blueberries and ate them.

Unfortunately, our lack of sleep caught up to us before we reached the crypt. A deep slumberous feeling overcame me, and I couldn't even muster the strength to take another step. I lay down in the mist and must have dozed off, because what happened next seemed like a dream.

I thought I saw the ghost dart over to us from where it had stood motionless among the statues. It had a freckled face, bright red lips, and green eyes that glowed like gemstones. Too tired to move, I cracked my eyes open a little wider and saw the count appear, looking at all of us while we slept.

"They ate the forbidden fruit," the ghost explained.

"Curses," Count Mirkea replied. "I told you to make a 'Do Not Touch the Fruit' sign a hundred years ago. You never obey me."

"I made that sign, but I put it in the kitchen."

"There is no fruit in the kitchen!" Count Mirkea hollered. "Allak, you are the most useless servant anyone could be cursed with!"

"There was a golden apple there," Allak argued. "It had the words 'for the fairest' written on it."

"I dug that up on St. George's Eve," the count replied. "It's a lost treasure from ancient Greece."

"Well, it was a fruit," Allak said. "That's why I put the sign there."

"Whatever happened to that apple?" Mirkea said. "It's not in my treasure trove in the tower."

"I took it," Allak said.

"What? But the sign said not to touch it!"

"But I'm the fairest," Allak replied. He blinked rapidly at the count and grinned widely. His perfect teeth sparkled between his bright red lips.

"Oh, you're impossible!" Count Mirkea complained. "Why did I ever buy this haunted castle? Anyway, you're not the fairest. I am."

Allak pulled a mirror out of some hidden pocket and said, "Mirror, Mirror, in my hand, who's the fairest in the land?"

"Why, you are, of course, Allak," the mirror replied, glowing briefly.

"That's my antique Persian hand mirror!" Count Mirkea yelled. "I dug that up, too! Where did you get that?"

"I took it from your treasure pile," Allak said.

"Who said you could raid my treasure trove?" Mirkea hollered.

"There wasn't any sign."

"Oh, my aching fangs," Count Mirkea said, putting his hands to his mouth. "You never finished that sign! Oh, never mind. Now throw these intruders off the cliff. I had other plans for them, but I just want to go back to bed."

"Can I do the riddle thing?" Allak asked. "I haven't done that in a long time."

"Fine," Count Mirkea said, handing Allak an antique

book with a gold clasp. "But make sure they don't enter my crypt. I need my beauty sleep. *And* I expect this book back. I dug it up a thousand years ago—it's my oldest treasure."

Suddenly, I woke up, and all my strength returned to me. I sat up right away. Allak and Count Mirkea were nowhere to be seen. Had it all been a dream? I scrambled to my feet and woke Paul.

"I had a weird dream," Paul mumbled, stretching out his arms and legs.

"Me too," I said. "C'mon, let's head into the crypt before something bad happens." That's when I noticed that Sean was missing. Had he been eaten by that blob that had been feasting on him? Bitten by a vampire? Thrown off the cliff?

"Sean, where are you?" Paul called out.

"Maybe he went down into the crypt ahead of us," I said. We ran toward the crypt, but when we approached the flaming torch, Allak suddenly appeared and held out his ghostly hand.

"Halt! You must answer three riddles in order to gain passage into the forbidden crypt," Allak said, holding the gold-clasped book in his other hand. So it hadn't been a dream at all! "Each time you miss an answer, one of the garden creatures will come to life and do what it does best!" He pointed at the various stone monstrosities that stood motionless in the graveyard.

"And what happens if we get a riddle right?" I asked.

"Um, I don't know, nobody's ever gotten one right." Allak unclasped the ancient book, wiped some dust off it, and opened to a yellow crinkly page. He cleared his throat and said, "Here is your first riddle: 'I am a word with three letters. Add two more, and there will be fewer. What word am I?'"

"*Less!*" Paul blurted, crossing his arms confidently.

"That has four letters!" I hollered. "What kind of a stupid answer was that?"

"Nope, the answer is *few*," Allak said. A low rumbling and the sound of crumbling stone came from the graveyard. The stone cow came to life and mooed softly, grazing on some weeds.

"How disappointing. Oh well, here is your second riddle," Allak said. "'At night they come without being fetched, and by day they are lost without being stolen. What are they?'"

"*Wolves!*" Paul shouted.

"Stop blurting out answers!" I said.

"Nope," Allak said. "*The stars.* Ha!" Another rumbling, crumbling sound came from the collection of statues, and this time the tiny stone frog came to life, said "Ribbit," and hopped over to us.

"You better hope you get the third riddle," Allak said, grimacing. I glanced over at the collection of frozen terrors, wondering which grisly beast might be the least harmful if it suddenly came to life. I shuddered at the thought of what the lizard knight would do to me with its big sword.

Suddenly, the frog leaped onto Allak's riddle book. He tried to shoo it away, swinging the book wildly. The frog jumped to safety, but the book hit the torch, immediately setting the brittle pages on fire. Allak desperately tried to blow on the fire, but ghosts don't have breath, so a few seconds later the book was a charred blob.

"The count will not be happy about this," Allak said. "No matter. I remember the third riddle. This is a classic one that the ancient Sphinx used to tell travelers: 'I have two eyes in the morning, two eyes at noon, and two eyes in the evening. What am I?'"

I put my hand over Paul's mouth and said, "Um, *a*

person, or almost any other living creature?"

"Uh, I guess so," Allak said, scratching his head. "I'm not sure I said that right."

A black cloud formed in the sky and released two bolts of lightning, one hitting the frog and the other zapping the cow. Their eyes began glowing. The frog, after releasing a deep, echoing "Ribbit," took one giant leap across the garden and landed on the cow, which immediately charged at Allak, whose eyes widened in surprise. He shrieked and ran, followed quickly by the rampaging cow and its small green passenger.

With the path into the crypt now clear, I grabbed the glowing torch, and Paul and I climbed down another flight of moss-covered stairs and entered a cold octagonal room. A large white spider was busy spinning a huge web across the entire ceiling. Icicles hung down, dripping into little puddles on the dirt floor. One unusually large icicle was broken off above a wooden coffin in the center of the room.

I tiptoed over to the coffin and found the edge of its dusty, rotting lid. I handed the torch to Paul and pushed the lid off, revealing Count Mirkea lying face up with his eyes wide open—yet he was fast asleep! Red liquid dripped from his lips, and he seemed less pale than before. My heart beat fast. Had he captured Sean and feasted on his blood while we were sleeping? Or were Lord Anddo and Shannz unable to prevent him from getting to Alice Grim in the tower?

"Look, the key ring," Paul whispered, pointing to Mirkea's waist.

Among a clutter of silver, gold, and jeweled keys was a big iron jail key. I carefully reached my hand onto the key and clutched it, trying to pull it over to a small gap in the ring where a key could be pulled out. As I slid it over, Count Mirkea's head suddenly turned sideways! I drew my hand back, but then I realized that he hadn't woken up. False alarm. With those round, glassy eyeballs staring at me, it was so hard to tell if he was sleeping. "I'll get it this time," I mumbled, reaching my hand back into the coffin.

"Hurry," Paul whispered.

I maneuvered the iron key out of the ring and gripped it in my hand. Suddenly, the wooden lid tilted away from the side of the coffin and hit the floor with a loud thud. Count Mirkea sat up, looked around, and said, "Allak, you fool!" He raised his hand, sending a stream of sharp icicles raining down from the ceiling. Paul and I dove away from two frozen spears just in time. The count glared at us with glowing red eyes as we scrambled to our feet and dashed for the door.

The Final Battle

As soon as we sprinted back up to the graveyard, a thunderous voice bellowed, "Who has dared to disturb the sleep of Count Mirkea?" A few stones tumbled off the side of the crypt and shattered on the ground.

"Let's hide in there," I said, pointing to a row of tall, neatly cut hedges with a gap in the side. A sloppy hand-painted sign read "The Never-Ending Hedge Maze—Voted Most Difficult Maze in the World by the London Institute of Hedges." As the sound of loud footsteps rose up from the crypt, we sprinted into the maze and darted around a bunch of twists and turns. The labyrinth extended down the steep mountainside into the valley below. Certain wrong turns led right off the edges of cliffs. We scrambled around corners and down bushy passageways without any strategy at all. It wasn't long before we were lost deep in the belly of the maze.

Soon the count began chanting in a strange language, and the words echoed across the valley, bouncing off the cliffs on both sides and growing so loud that it hurt my eardrums. Thousands of bats flew out of the hedges and formed a swirling black mass in the sky, making it as dark as night. Wolves, werewolves, and dragons clamored in the distance.

"Do you think Count Mirkea knows his way around this place?" I asked as we tumbled down a steep incline and crashed against a hedge wall. A fireball shot up from the direction of the graveyard, expanded to fill the sky, and transformed into a giant flaming bat. In one shrieking power dive, it engulfed the hedges, scorching them instantly as it sped toward us.

"Duck!" Paul cried. We dove to the ground and flattened ourselves as the giant flamebat zoomed over us and disappeared into the valley. When we stood up, we were surrounded by the charred ashes of the once great hedge maze. An old lady walked nearby, muttering softly to herself.

"You're almost out of the maze, Hilda, almost out," she said. "After thirty-seven years of wandering, you'll be going home now." She climbed over the ash piles and hobbled up the steep path toward the castle.

The count stood on a rocky crag above us, his body glowing in sharp contrast to the black castle behind him.

"Which one of you stole my tower key?" he said in a gravelly tone.

"He did," Paul and I said, pointing at each other. Then I looked down. I was still clutching the key.

Count Mirkea chanted another strange phrase, and right away the bats swooped down and surrounded us, clutching our clothes with sharp claws. As they lifted us high in the air, Paul desperately clung onto his backpack. I could see the Honus Wagner card through a little hole that the wolves had made when they chewed on it. Would I ever get a chance to hold it again in the safety of home?

The bats soared up and around the tower, eventually taking us through an unbarred window and depositing us next to Alice Grim inside the prison cell. As soon as we hit the ground, a rat snatched the jail key away from me and disappeared into a hole in the wall. Then a bright red bat flew through the same window, fluttered through the jail door, and hovered next to Lord Anddo and Shannz. The red bat transformed into Count Mirkea, who glared at me and Paul.

"I knew you were evil!" I cried. "Why didn't you just capture us right away instead of toying with us like you did?"

"I thought perhaps you would like to be my friends," Count Mirkea said, brushing himself off. "I treated you well, but you performed the first acts of treachery by interrupting my sleep and stealing my key!"

"Did you want Alice to be your friend, too?" I said, suddenly noticing that she didn't have her garlic bag anymore. She clutched her wooden doll with trembling hands.

"No, she's *lunch*," Count Mirkea said, snapping his fingers. "But now I have a full-course supper right in this very room!" The rat darted out of another hole and delivered the prison key to Count Mirkea, who quickly opened the prison door and gestured for Lord Anddo and Shannz to enter the cell.

Lord Anddo extended both arms, pointed at the count, and closed his eyes. The count was slammed backward against the wall and slid to the ground, tearing his cape on the sharp stones. Mirkea scowled at Lord Anddo and held out his hand, sending him and Shannz flying into the prison cell. The door immediately slammed shut behind them.

"Did you see that?" Lord Anddo said, jumping to his feet. "I smashed him against the wall! Maybe Mom's prophecy was right—I have to spend more time with Sis to fulfill my true destiny." He examined his hands while Shannz rolled her eyes.

"All you care about is power," Shannz said. "Don't you realize the situation we're in?"

"Yeah, and I'm trying to do something about it," Lord Anddo said, holding out his hand toward the count again. Outside the cell, Count Mirkea flinched a little as he set up a wooden table and placed an iron bowl and spoon on it. Then he assembled a cot next to the table.

"Well, who wants to be the appetizer?" Count Mirkea said, putting on a paper bib covered with images of red lobsters. "It's not so bad. Just think, you'll dwell among the undead for all eternity. No takers?" He pointed his arm at me, and I began floating toward the prison door, which creaked open, allowing me to waft out and land gently on the cot.

"Sean!" I cried out, unable to move my arms or legs. "Where are you? We need help up here!"

The count rubbed some antiseptic on my neck and then leaned down so close that I could feel his icy breath and the touch of his cold nose on my neck. Then his sharp teeth touched up against my skin. I closed my eyes, wondering what it would be like to be an undead vampire. Would I have to drink blood, or could really saucy pizza count?

"I'm right here," Sean said, carrying a large silver tray up the tower stairs. He stepped onto the landing, put the tray on the table, and pulled the lid off, revealing a frozen mound of ice cream with red sauce dripping off it.

"What is that concoction?" Count Mirkea asked, pulling his mouth away from my neck without taking a bite. "It doesn't appear to be a solid or a liquid."

"It's ice cream," Sean said, "with a very special syrup made just for you."

"Is it blood?" Count Mirkea asked, swiping his finger toward it. Sean slapped his hand away.

"I brought serving bowls. We'll eat like civilized people." He spooned the ice cream into bowls. Count Mirkea grabbed his and gulped down large spoonfuls, slurping up the red liquid that dripped onto his chin.

"It's good!" he said, grabbing the serving tray and jamming his face into it to devour the rest. As the count became a sticky, gooey mess, I realized that I could move my arms and legs again, so I slowly got up from the cot and backed away from it.

Moments later Count Mirkea's smile disappeared, and he held his stomach, wincing in pain. Sean smiled widely.

"What trickery is this?" Count Mirkea said, groaning. "I've been poisoned!" He fell to his knees, his skin turned wrinkly, and his hair began falling out.

"You're no match for my tricky smarts!" Sean said, blowing on his fingers.

Count Mirkea raised his right hand, creating a huge bolt of lightning that zapped through the tower roof, sending broken stones tumbling into the prison cells. His other hand created a swirling whirlwind that quickly devoured the tower staircase, causing it to tumble far below with a thunderous crash. The ancient tower began teetering.

"I know I'll get blamed for this," Allak the ghost said, peeking in through the gaping hole in the ceiling. One large stone tumbled into the treasure room and knocked over the sign that read "Please Do Not."

"Allak, you fool," Count Mirkea said weakly, lying on the ground. "You couldn't scare off a plague rat. Now where's that ancient book I lent you? There's a chant in there that could cure me."

"Um, the book burned a little," Allak said.

"How little?" Mirkea muttered weakly.

"A lot."

"Curses." Mirkea spread out his arms and transformed again into a red bat, fluttering around erratically. It stuck a long tongue out at Allak and then disappeared in a puff of smoke.

"Hurry, you must leave the tower," Allak said. "I've knocked over other towers in the castle, so I know this one won't stand much longer." The ghost floated into the treasure room and grabbed an armful of golden objects.

"Help, Allak," I said frantically as the roof came loose above us, slid off the side, and shattered with a cacophonous boom in the courtyard below. Open sky surrounded us. Swarms of frightened bats shrieked and fled into the distance. Below, I could hear the innards of the tower disintegrating, the ancient stones coming loose and pulverizing under their own weight. We had only moments before our high-up platform tumbled in a horrible free fall.

"I would carry you, but my arms are full," Allak replied, flying into the stormy sky above the disintegrating tower. He sped off to a distant part of the castle.

As the floor began splitting apart below us, Alice Grim jumped into Shannz's arms. Suddenly, Cybrax, glowing bright green, burst through one of the crumbling walls, its microchips beeping wildly.

"All aboard," it announced. We dove onto the surfboard, which stretched itself out to accommodate the whole group. Just as we launched into the gloomy sky, the entire tower fell over and shattered into a cloud of rock dust. The crashing sound was drowned out by thunder that rumbled all around us.

As Shannz held on to Alice and Lord Anddo held on to his sister and I clutched Paul's backpack, the surfboard sped over the cliff and into the valley. I thought I saw Allak wave to us from a castle window as we zoomed down and surfed from treetop to treetop. When Cybrax reached the far end of the valley, it surfed straight up the cliff wall and into a black cloud. We went up so fast that we all scattered off the

board—my mouth got stuck in a permanent scream as we whizzed down toward the forest—but then Cybrax zipped around and caught everyone.

"I feel so alive!" Cybrax cheered as a nauseated feeling welled up inside me.

"Stop showing off and fly us to the Bistritz Hotel!" Shannz said.

"How in the world did you make ice cream in a castle without electricity?" Paul asked Sean as we soared gently over the treetops.

"And how did it defeat Count Mirkea?" I added.

"It was easy," Sean said. "When I woke up in the graveyard before you fellas did, I went down into the crypt and found all those icicles. I broke off the biggest one, and then I ran back up and collected a whole bunch of strawberries from the bushes. I went to the kitchen and mashed them all together, but it just turned into an icy mush. That's when I realized that I had forgotten the most important ingredient—milk! When I got back to the graveyard, you guys were gone, but there was a rampaging cow with a frog and Allak on its back. So I milked the cow, and then Allak flew me back to the kitchen so I could add the milk to the strawberry ice mush. Then I convinced Allak to fly through the tower window and steal the bag of garlic from Alice Grim—I just told him he would get to have all the treasure if he did. I made raspberry garlic syrup for the final touch!"

"Brilliant," Shannz said.

"I know, I know," Sean said. "I'm really the genius type, but I like to be modest about it."

"Coming in for a landing at the Bistritz Hotel," Cybrax said. "Thank you for flying Air Cybrax." We glided gently down toward an inn nestled in the treetops.

I Tell You About the Resolution

When we landed at the Bistritz Hotel, Alice was immediately reunited with her overjoyed parents. The rest
of us were treated like freakish superpowered heroes
again. Mobs of people surrounded us, asking us all
sorts of questions, mostly in a foreign language. Some
of the women made weird signs with their hands, saying
"vrolok" and "todten" over and over again, then pointing to the ruined castle far away on the hillside. I could
only guess that meant "vampire" or "evil boy."

"May I try your flying machine?" one boy asked,
pulling on my shirt.

"Did you battle the vrolok?" another asked. "We saw
and heard lightning and thunder across the valley."

"That vampire won't be terrorizing these mountains
anymore," I said, "although there's a ghost that you
may need to worry about." Some of the kids looked at
me with wide eyes.

"Here, I want you to have this as thanks for saving

me," Alice said, handing her wooden doll to Sean. He tried to refuse her offer, but Alice forced it into his hands. "You can remember me whenever you play with her."

"Um, I guess I'll be remembering you a lot, then," Sean said sarcastically, holding the doll away from himself awkwardly.

Desperate to get away from the mobs, we hopped onto Cybrax and sped to a remote part of the Carpathian Mountains—a jagged stone jutting out over the valley, inaccessible by foot. That's where we planned the last phase of our journey—getting everybody home.

"Do you think we fixed the future?" Sean asked.

"Who knows?" Paul replied, flipping through the TimeQuest 2 comic. "No more comic panels have filled in."

"And Answer Box can answer questions only about the past or present," I added.

"True dat, true dat," Answer Box replied from Shannz's pocket.

"But how can we get home?" Lord Anddo asked, looking at his computerized bracelet. "Remember the TimeQuest rules?"

"If you get a brand-new TimeQuest 2 comic, you can go anywhere again," Shannz said. "Remember when you shut down the TimeQuest factory? You dumped all their unused comics in a big mound on Refuse Beach. I hid them safely in a distant time period, where nobody could mess around with them—and where I could get them whenever I wanted."

"Pretty sneaky, Sis," Lord Anddo said. "What year did you hide them in?"

"I won't tell unless you grant me three wishes," Shannz said.

"What do I look like, a genie?" Lord Anddo complained. "You want to go home just as badly as me!"

"My first wish is that when we return home, I want to live with you in the energy sphere and help you rule the world."

"OK, forget that, let's hear your second wish," Lord Anddo said.

"Apparently, your silly little powers emerge only when I'm around," Shannz said, sitting down and crossing her legs. "We'll stay here until you agree to it." Anddo sat down with his back to Shannz, and they didn't say anything for a while. Meanwhile, the rest of us stood around and tapped our feet or whistled.

"All right, fine," Lord Anddo said, standing up. "You can come live with me, but you're not just gonna surf all day if you do. You're gonna help me—ruling the world is hard work!"

"And for my second wish, I want Mom and Dad to come live with us, too," Shannz continued, standing up and smiling.

"WHAT!" Lord Anddo said, pulling on his hair. "But they'll tell me what time to go to bed and stuff.

That'll be awful."

Shannz sat down again and crossed her legs.

"Fine!" Lord Anddo said. "You win. Let's just go home."

"Bracelet," Shannz began, "take us to the year 2 billion B.C. next to the big mound of TimeQuest 2 comics by Pinnacle Rock."

"Preparing to warp the space-time continuum," the bracelet announced. After a brief zap and momentary dizziness, we appeared on a barren landscape filled with clear water and hardened lava. An oversized orange sun glared at us from the horizon. A giant teetering mound of TimeQuest 2 comics stood next to a large red boulder that pointed to the sky like an arrowhead.

"It worked!" I said, suddenly noticing a purple coin on the ground. I picked it up and handed it to Lord Anddo.

"Thanks," he said, snatching it. "Now you owe me only one octillion, two hundred seventy-one septillion—"

"And for my third wish," Shannz interrupted, pulling a couple of TimeQuest 2 comics off the pile, "I want you to forget the debt that these boys owe you."

"Now you're pushing it, Sis," Lord Anddo said. "Just because they saved the world doesn't mean—" Shannz crossed her arms again. "Oh, fine. I already have so much money I had to put it on an asteroid anyway. The debt is forgiven." Shannz smiled.

It would be exciting to tell you that we got attacked by a giant paramecium or something in super-prehistoric times, but there wasn't any big life on Earth back then, so all that happened was Shannz handed a TimeQuest 2 comic to Sean and kept another for herself. Then there was a lot of mushy hugging and good-byes and all that stuff, and everybody warped home—Sean to 1912 so he could disembark from the *Titanic*; Shannz and Lord Anddo to the year 100,000 on Earth 2; Paul and I back to Springs in 2002.

We appeared back on my bedroom floor, exactly where we had started the journey in the first place. I immediately kissed my carpet, thrilled and amazed that we had successfully saved the world! I looked at the clock—it was only a few minutes after we had left on the journey, the night we played Pictionary with Mom and Dad.

"We fixed things!" Paul exclaimed.

"Do we still have it?" I asked, diving for Paul's backpack. I pulled out the Honus Wagner card, still in mint condition inside its beaten-up plastic case. It was glossy and new-looking, with Honus's signature as bright as the day it was made. Excited, I spread out a white sheet and transferred it into a brand-new plastic case. Then I held it up to the light, where we admired the one-million-dollar card.

"I can't believe we made it back with the card," Paul said. "And we saved the *Titanic* and took care of Dracula, or his cousin or something. We're really getting good at this time-travel thing!"

"C'mon, let's go show this card to my dad. He's gonna flip out." We ran downstairs into the den, where Mom and Dad were quietly reading magazines. As a burst of excitement raced through me, I tiptoed over to Dad and slowly placed the Honus Wagner card on his lap.

"What's this?" Dad asked.

"It's a replacement Honus Wagner card from 1909!" I announced. "This is the one with Honus's signature, the one that Grandma Mattie wrote about in her diary!"

"I do recall reading something about a baseball card in Mattie's diary," Dad said. "Where did you find that? Is it valuable?"

"It's worth a million dollars!" I said, confused. I had expected him to act more surprised.

"I doubt a card could be worth that much," Dad said.

"Don't you remember, when I was four I ate the Honus Wagner card that Grandma Mattie had given you," I said frantically. "It was your most prized possession. Now I've replaced it, and everything's back to normal!"

"That was Grandma Mattie's wooden doll you ate," Mom chimed in. "You bit its head off while Dad was cleaning it on his bed one day. We never could understand why a four-year-old boy would want to eat a doll's head. You nearly choked on chunks of splintered wood."

"What! Another change!" I said angrily. "How could that be possible? I'm sick of this time-travel-but-terfly-effect-changing-the-future junk! Well, who cares if I ate a doll? This card's worth a million dollars. We could sell it and buy a thousand dolls."

"Not that doll," Dad said. "It was handmade in England in the 1700s, supposedly for a royal princess. It was one of a kind."

"Fine, but we still have a million dollars," I said, holding the plastic case right up to his face. "Dad, you can retire early, just like you've always wanted to." Dad glanced at the card, then back up at me.

"It looks brand-new," he said.

"Let's go get the price guide and show him," I said to Paul impatiently. We immediately ran back upstairs and found the baseball-card price guide, the one Paul had written "Cheer up, homey" on before we left on our adventure. Oddly, Paul's writing was not on the cover anymore. I flipped to the section on the world's most valuable baseball cards. The Honus Wagner card wasn't on the list!

"What's going on?" I asked Paul frantically.

"We must have changed something when we were messing with time," Paul said, flipping through Mattie's diary. "Listen to this entry where Mattie talked about the Honus Wagner card that she gave to your dad." Paul read me the page from the diary:

"May 29, 1940

Dear Diary:

Today Father gave me a rare doll as a present. It is handmade from ancient wood, constructed using the highest standards of quality. Supposedly it was once owned by an English princess in the 1700s! Father acquired the doll from my uncle Sean, who had received it as a gift during a trip to Europe he had taken with his mother, Esmerelda. (Oh, Diary, they even sailed home on the grand steamship the Titanic—*the largest ocean liner in the world!) Father told me to take good care of the doll because it has special magical powers.*

Although I begged and pleaded, Father would not tell me what powers the doll has. He told me only that he traded a popular baseball card for it when he was just twelve years old. Now I know my father, and he wouldn't trade a baseball card for a doll unless it really did have powers. I named the doll Esmerelda, after my grandmother. I will pass it down to my children, and they their children, all the way down through eternity … or at least until some fool child bites its head off.

I have decided to give up my hobby of baseball-card collecting in favor of doll collecting. Dolls are much more companionable than small pieces of

cardboard, and you can play with them all day long.
I may even make a house for Esmerelda. Oh, Diary,
what a happy day this was!"

"I don't believe it," I said, slapping my face. "When he got back home, Sean traded Alice Grim's doll for a Honus Wagner card, to replace the card he gave to us!"

"He got the one his brother had, the one without the signature!" Paul added. "So it was never passed on to Mattie and your dad. I wonder whatever happened to it."

"Well, it doesn't matter, because according to this price guide, the card isn't worth a whole lot anymore."

"How much is it worth?" Paul asked.

I flipped to the tobacco-card section to locate the specific listing on the 1909 Honus Wagner card. Surprisingly, there was a whole paragraph about the card!

The 1909 Honus Wagner T206 card has much lore, rumor, and history connected to it. At first only a few of these cards were ever released because Honus Wagner objected to having his name connected with anything sold inside tobacco products. However, in 1912, the young Sean Talmage, then famous for his ability to predict the future, told the world that this card would be worth a million dollars some day. Naturally, everybody flocked to get one, and the few Honus Wagner cards that existed were stashed away in mint condition, until the day that they might become as valuable as the boy predicted. The company released an additional 15,000 cards that it had printed in 1909 (and were apparently stored in the factory's basement and destined to be destroyed). They were sold inside packages of gum instead of tobacco. Today, thousands of these cards are available on the market, still in mint condition, making the Honus Wagner card readily available and the least valuable of any tobacco card ever printed.

"We're ruined!" I said. "Now we're right back where we started."

"Well, we did save the *Titanic* from sinking," Paul said as he wrote "Cheer up, homey" again in bright yellow marker on my baseball-card price guide.

"Yeah, but my original plan failed. My dad still hates me!"

I Learn the Truth

The next day in Mr. O's English class, things got even more bizarre. We read a nonfiction piece about some of the more eccentric presidents of the United States and their weird habits. Paul sat next to me, and we looked at each other in shock when Mr. O handed us an article entitled "President Sean Talmage and the Squash Affair." The article read:

> President Sean Talmage, the thirty-third president of the United States, was perhaps the most eccentric of all U.S. presidents. He was president from 1945–1953 and most remembered for his vigorous antisquash campaign. Under his rule, all squash in the United States was eliminated, making it the first vegetable ever eradicated by a U.S. president. When vegetable-rights activists protested across the country, Sean used taxpayer dollars to build an underwater base, where he hid out until things cooled down.

Although the country called for impeachment, his hatred of squash actually served a useful purpose. On August 6, 1945, President Talmage ordered one million tons of squash dropped on the city of Hiroshima, ending Japanese involvement in World War II. The soft vegetable did not cause any injuries, but extreme disgust caused an immediate surrender on the part of the Japanese.

A few days later, in a radio address, President Talmage credited his good leadership skills to a boy from the year 100,000, who ruled a planetoid known as Earth 2. The president said that the boy taught him all the secrets to being a good ruler. Shortly after this radio address, President Talmage was admitted to a mental institution, but he escaped and hid out in his underwater base until things cooled down.

This was not the first time that President Talmage had made an eccentric claim. He had already been famous from childhood for saving the Titanic *steamship from sinking in the North Atlantic with the help of so-called "visitors from the future." His claim of futuristic intervention was never substantiated, leading to speculation of a massive cover-up by the White Star Line. Still, President Talmage became famous for his ability to predict events that hadn't yet occurred.*

"All these changes, but we didn't get anything good out of this whole journey," I whispered to Paul. He shrugged while Mr. O glared at me for talking in class. I was starting to think that TimeQuest 2 Inc. had something against me personally.

"At least we saved Hiroshima," Paul muttered back. "I guess Sean became president instead of Harry Truman."

"Wait a minute. I know what we can do!" I shrieked, suddenly remembering something that the Answer Box had told us. Mr. O stopped talking and looked at me angrily. I quickly shut up and wrote out a note to Paul instead.

Paul—

I just remembered, Answer Box once said there wuz a buried treasure in the Kmart parking lot, fifty yards south of the entrance! All we have to do iz convince the Kmart peeps 2 let us dig a hole thru the pavement and then we'll B rich!

—Bri

Later that day I tried to convince Mom and Dad to take me to Kmart. They agreed that we needed to go shopping for some stuff, but they gave me and Paul strange looks when we brought along a shovel and Paul's old metal detector. While Mom and Dad went inside the store, Paul and I counted out fifty yards south of the entrance. Amazingly, my counting ended at a grassy island in the middle of the parking lot. Paul swung his metal detector over the grass, and it immediately gave out a loud beep. Treasure!

"I'll dig, you keep a lookout," I said. "The Answer Box said it was three feet under the ground."

"Look out for what?" Paul asked. "There are people all around."

"Fine. Then we'll just tell them we're landscapers," I said, scooping up a chunk of dirt and grass.

"That would be lying, I believe," Paul said sarcastically.

"Be quiet. There are millions of dollars under here."

I dug and dug until there was a big mound of dirt next to Paul. Whenever anybody walked by, he tried to stand in front of me to block their view, but he's too skinny, so people gave me strange looks anyway. When Mom and Dad came out holding a bunch of bags, I had already dug down about two feet.

"Brian, what are you doing?" Dad hollered.

"Digging for treasure," I said, embarrassed.

"In a parking lot?" Mom screamed. "This isn't our property. We'll have to pay for this!"

Just then my shovel slammed against something metallic. I cleared away a little dirt and saw a corner of a chest. My heart started racing as Paul tried to help me clear enough dirt off to lift the thing out of the ground. Mom and Dad stopped yelling and looked on curiously. Soon, other passersby stopped and watched us clear away enough dirt to reveal a tarnished brass treasure chest. Finally, our adventure was about to pay off! Dad might still hate me for destroying his most prized possession, but this treasure chest would change everything. I imagined the mounds of gleaming gold that lay inside.

A bunch of people helped us lift the heavy thing out of the hole. After it slammed against the ground, I cleared the dirt away from the latch. I opened the creaky lid while everybody leaned over my shoulder. There wasn't any gleaming gold inside at all—just an old, yellowish piece of paper. I picked it up and read it:

Dear Brian and Paul:

I bet you fellas thought I forgot where the treasure was buried, didn't you? Ha! Don't forget about my tricky smarts. When I warped back home to 1912, I became world famous for helping to save the Titanic. *Remember that doll that Alice Grim had given me? I convinced my brother that it had powers so he would trade me the other Honus Wagner card for it. Well, he didn't believe me right away, but then I said that the doll told me where a great treasure was buried. So we went to dig it up, and we actually found it! Lots of chests of gold and jewels, and some old scrolls from like 3,000 B.C. or something. Then he believed me! Anyway, I traded away that dumb doll, and now I have my Honus Wagner card again, only it doesn't have the signature anymore. Oh, sorry I didn't leave any treasure for you. I need it to fund my political campaign when I get older.*

Sincerely,

Sean Talmage
(future ruler of the world)

"I can't win!" I screamed, ripping up the note and tossing it in the hole.

"What did you just do?" a lady said to me. "That looked

like a vintage note from President Talmage when he was a child. It had his signature on it and must have been worth thousands." I buried my face in my dirty hands and began crying while everybody around me groaned.

Later that day, we read the TimeQuest 2 comic up in my bedroom one last time. The entire book had filled in, down to the very last page. The colorful comic panels showed our awkward dinner with Count Mirkea, the descent into the forbidden crypt, Allak's riddles, a giant fireball engulfing the hedge maze, our final encounter with Count Mirkea in the prison, Cybrax's dramatic rescue when the tower collapsed, and our trip to 2 billion B.C. to get new TimeQuest 2 comics that Shannz had stashed there.

196

A caption read, "By preventing Alice Grim from getting bitten by the vampire, our heroes have saved the world from certain doom. Alice will now grow up to be a lawyer and will never create that horrible mutation that overtook Earth. The journey is over for our young heroes, and everybody will live happily ever after!" A circle on the last page showed Sean reunited with Esmerelda. A speech bubble came out of Sean's mouth, saying, "Look, Ma, my Miasma Corrosus is cured!" Another circle showed Anddo, Shannz, and their parents living together inside a bigger, better energy sphere on Earth 2. The final circle showed me with a sad look on my face. The caption read, "But what about Brian? After all that work, he still wonders whether his dad hates him for destroying his most valuable possession—a handmade one-of-a-kind wooden doll from the eighteenth century! What should he do now?"

Suddenly, a holographic boy jumped out at me from the back cover and said, "Perhaps a brand-new TimeQuest 2 comic adventure will fix things! You and Paul can warp to ancient Greece and bring back some gold coins, or zap to Atlantis and acquire a rare scroll; perhaps spend some time with seventeenth-century pirates in the Caribbean, or take a trip to Mars and bring back some extraterrestrial rocks to sell on eBay. If you need money, then what better way to get it than with the boundless treasure-hunting possibilities provided by TimeQuest 2?" The boy winked at me.

Then a holographic girl appeared and said quickly, "We regret to inform you that TimeQuest 2 comics are no longer available for purchase due to Lord Anddo's seizing of the company. We are sorry for the inconvenience." The boy looked at the girl with disappointment, and then they both disappeared.

"I got it!" I said, snapping my fingers. "We'll use our TimeQuest bracelets to go back to 2 billion B.C. and get more TimeQuest 2 comics from that big pile. Then we'll go all over the world collecting treasures from various time periods, and then my dad can retire."

"Good idea. How come we didn't take back a whole pile of them when we were there?" Paul asked. "Only we can't go back to 2 billion B.C. because we've already been there using these bracelets."

"So! We can warp to 1 billion B.C.—what's the difference? Nobody was around back then to mess with these comics. They should still be in the same place!"

"I dunno," Paul said. "I'm kinda tired. Sleepovers with you usually don't involve much sleep."

Suddenly, the bracelet on my wrist began beeping, and the words "Thank you for using TimeQuest merchandise—comic completed" scrolled across the miniature screen. Then the bracelet disappeared! A few seconds later, Paul's disappeared too!

"So much for that idea," Paul said. "I'm going to bed." He flopped onto my bottom bunk and fell asleep almost immediately.

"Won't anything go right?" I cried, tossing the TimeQuest 2 comic on the floor. The title immediately changed from "TimeQuest 2" to "The Baseball Card Kid—a one-issue adventure." The magical, ever-changing pictures on the cover now showed various scenes from our adventures. Feeling utterly hopeless, I shut off my light and climbed up to my top bunk. A few minutes later the door creaked open, and someone tiptoed over to my bed.

"Dad?"

"What's gotten into you lately, Brian?" Dad asked. "Mom and I have been worried. You spend all your time with Paul, strange packages arrive in the mail, our mailbox gets struck by lightning, you dig up the Kmart parking lot, we receive a note from Mr. O saying that you've been distracted in class, and you've been going on and on about some baseball card. Can you explain any of this?"

"Dad, Paul and I have been trying to replace your most valuable possession for over a year now. First it was a *Superman #1* comic book, then it was a Honus Wagner baseball card, and now it's a rare doll. But something always goes wrong. I just want you to be able to have a million dollars, so you can retire, like you planned to do before I wrecked everything."

"I don't want to retire," Dad said. "I like my job. Did I say I wanted to?"

"You said it when I was four," I answered. "And then

you never told me another treasure chest story after I wrecked your most prized possession."

"That's because my hours at work shifted right after that," Dad said. "I came home too late, and you were already asleep. Don't you remember? I went back to regular hours only two years ago, and I thought at eleven you were too old for bedtime stories."

"Oh."

"If you want I can tell you stories again. I had no idea that was part of the problem."

"I always wanted to hear the one about the mad scientist that turned boys into monkeys."

"Oh, that's a classic," Dad said, clearing his throat. "Once upon a time there was a mad scientist who lived on a deserted island in the middle of the Pacific." I curled up in bed under the covers, just like I did when I was little. A few seconds later, I fell asleep.